DEATH AT THE OLD CURIOSITY SHOP

THE COTSWOLD CURIOSITY SHOP MYSTERIES

DEBBIE YOUNG

Boldwood

First published in Great Britain in 2024 by Boldwood Books Ltd.

Cover Design by Lizzie Gardiner

Cover Illustration: Shutterstock

A CIP catalogue record for this book is available from the British Library.

Paperback ISBN 978-1-83518-554-4

Large Print ISBN 978-1-83518-550-6

Hardback ISBN 978-1-83518-549-0

Ebook ISBN 978-1-83518-547-6

Kindle ISBN 978-1-83518-548-3

Audio CD ISBN 978-1-83518-555-1

MP3 CD ISBN 978-1-83518-552-0

Digital audio download ISBN 978-1-83518-546-9

Boldwood Books Ltd
23 Bowerdean Street
London SW6 3TN
www.boldwoodbooks.com

To Alison Morton

1

FAST FORWARD

What could be more idyllic than moving out of the bustling city centre of Broadwick to the peaceful Cotswold village of Little Pride? Every building there is a luscious concoction of honey-coloured stone. Gorgeous cottage gardens overflow with lilac and lavender, apple blossom and foxgloves. So, that fateful spring day, when I had the opportunity to buy a tumbledown old home at a bargain price, I embraced it as exactly the fresh start I needed. Little did I realise that in Little Pride, nothing is ever quite as it seems.

I thought I knew exactly the right question to ask young Miles Swansong, the estate agent, and he gave me the answers I wanted to hear. I was particularly pleased when he confirmed the village was in an Area of Outstanding Natural Beauty. This means the local council's planning department has particularly strict rules to ensure it remains unspoiled.

Whenever you want to repair or extend your house, or to build new homes, you must seek the council's permission, at your own expense, with no guarantee that it will be granted. It's therefore important to keep on good terms with the council's planning department – especially when you're planning a major overhaul on an old property, as I was, turning a former shop into a cosy cottage home.

So, finding the body of one of its officers sprawled across the tea table on my front terrace was unfortunate to say the least. Wrapped around her throat was a tie-dyed scarf that I didn't remember her wearing earlier. In her hand was a bunch of cow parsley, and in the other an old-fashioned, hexagonal, blue bottle with the word *POISON* embossed down one side.

The only dead bodies I'd ever seen before had been much more tidily presented – the fine collection of Egyptian mummies, donated by Edwardian tomb-raiders to the city museum where I used to work. The mummies were bandaged as neatly as if it were done by Girl Guides training for their First Aid badge. No one had gift-wrapped this body. Which, to my surprise, turned out to be just as well.

Let me take you back to how it all started...

2

THE LIE OF THE LAND

The fact that the estate agent trying to sell me the cottage looked about twelve years old should have rung alarm bells. But having just hit fifty, I was used to working with younger people, so I didn't think to question his ability.

It had been a quarter of a century since I'd bought what I thought would be our forever home with my then partner Steven. At the time, we'd felt rather smug. Having met in Freshers' Week at university at a History Society party, our common interest in the past had quickly forged a firm bond between us. I was hugely into the Victorians, the era I eventually specialised in for my history degree, and Steven, a law student, had a hobbyist's interest in historical arts and crafts.

Our shared passion for visiting museums and stately homes, when our peers were more interested in pubs and clubs, made us feel terribly grown-up. It also convinced me that I'd found my soulmate. When our friends teased us for being prematurely middle-aged, I laughed it off, dismissing them as jealous and immature. I thought I'd had the last laugh, becoming a homeowner (albeit with a huge mortgage and a deposit saved by depriving ourselves of a social life and holidays as soon as we started earning), while they were still flat-sharing and sofa-surfing, student style. My parents, seeing me follow in their footsteps as a middle-class urban house-holder, although on the other side of the country from their home in Tunbridge Wells, were terribly pleased and proud.

Having got onto the property ladder at the age of twenty-five, we planned to pay off our mortgage and own our home outright before we hit our half-century. From that point forward, we planned to spend our disposable income on fun stuff such as travel and enter-tainment. I'd never have guessed that within mere months of making the last payment on our mortgage, I'd be house hunting once more, and that this time, I'd be on my own.

When I booked the viewing, I'd made it clear that my partner was a lawyer. I thought that ought to mark me out as someone who knew what they were doing when buying a house – a client not to be messed with. Well, ex-partner, actually, but Swansong and Sons didn't need to know that. Nor did they need to know that Steven's expertise wasn't in conveyancing, but in trademark law.

It would be easy for me to blame the estate agent for much of what went wrong. Not for the criminal assault on the planning offi-cer, of course, but for his spectacular ineptitude. I must have been his dream client – an eager cash buyer in a hurry, with no chain albeit with only half the value of the house we had just sold. He told me what I wanted to hear, and I didn't realise the many errors he had made until long after I'd moved in. I should have been more careful and vigilant, especially when I could see he was so young and inexperienced.

My first mistake was to trust Miles when he said he could fast track me into the home of my dreams, if only I'd be a little flexible about my requirements. He was a smooth talker, persuading me to consider moving further afield than I'd originally planned. After living in the city for so long, the idea of more space for my money and fresh country air appealed to me. When Steven and I parted, I'd assumed I'd have to downsize from our urban, Edwardian, terraced house. So, when Miles told me that if I moved a mere twenty miles from the city centre, I could buy a whole house, I couldn't resist.

That's how, in the middle of May, I came to be standing on the high street of a quiet village in the Cotswolds, clutching the particulars of a quaint Victorian cottage. *Nell Little's Cotswold Curiosity Shop* announced the peeling, hand-painted, wooden board above the bay window at the front of the house.

'Cute name,' I commented to Miles, although I suspected the Dickensian reference would be lost on him. 'If I were to buy it, I'd rename it Curiosity Cottage to preserve its heritage as a former shop. That should stand me in good stead with my new neighbours. It would look good on a change of address card too.'

When Miles stared at me blankly, I realised that his generation might not know what change of address cards were. They'd just post on WhatsApp or Snapchat or whatever the latest fad was for keeping tabs on your mates. Miles might have been half my age, but he was making me feel twice mine.

'I'd better not buy a cat, though,' I quipped, trying to joke my way out of my embarrassment.

'Why, are you allergic to cats?' he asked in tones of practised politeness. I expect Mr Swansong Senior had coached young Miles in making polite conversation with strangers as part of his training. 'I'm allergic to mushrooms,' he continued conversationally. 'They bring me out in a rash.'

He was probably doing his best to find common ground with me, so I tried to banter with him, to use a Gen Z term.

'Don't worry, I wouldn't plan to eat the cat.'

He gasped and took a step backwards, clutching his electronic tablet to his chest. You'd have thought I'd just told him I was a cannibal.

'No, no, that's a joke,' I added hastily. 'You know the old saying: curiosity killed the cat.'

From his reply, it was clear that he didn't, but at least he tried to enter into the spirit of things.

'I suppose it would if the cat was curious enough to climb into a washing machine and you closed the door and turned it on and didn't notice.'

'No!' I glanced around, hoping my shriek of horror at his suggestion hadn't frightened my potential new neighbours. I'd heard Cotswold villages can be reluctant to welcome outsiders. I didn't want to alienate them before I'd even moved in.

If I moved in. What was I thinking?

'Please, forget about the cats,' I begged. 'Just tell me everything you know about this property.' I stepped back to the kerb to better appraise the front of the house. Considering the cottage had been standing empty for some months, it didn't look too bad. 'Firstly, is it listed?'

Miles stood up a little straighter, pressed a button on his tablet, and waited for a file to load.

'No, it's not listed in any way, apart from on our company website, ha ha.' I suspect he'd been fed that quip as part of his training. His tablet gave a cheery ping, and he read from the screen. 'Its price has recently been lowered to a more realistic level to facilitate a faster sale. I know you don't want to hang around, given you've already sold your current property, and there are no other parties involved in associated transactions so its immediate availability would suit your particular need.'

'You mean there's no chain to delay the sale, and I can have vacant possession?'

If he'd cut to the chase instead of waffling, he'd have speeded up the sale process.

I crossed the Cotswold stone slabs that formed the hardstanding in front of the cottage and peered through the grimy window into the cluttered front room, once home to Nell Little's shop.

'It doesn't look very vacant to me,' I observed.

I pulled a tissue from my pocket, and, keeping my back to Miles so he couldn't see what I was doing, I spat on it and scrubbed a clean spyhole. Well, relatively clean, if you don't count my spit.

An old-fashioned wooden counter ran around two sides of the little room, with floor-to-ceiling shelves behind. Every flat space was filled with a mish-mash of objects of all shapes and sizes, from a china trinket dish overflowing with enamel badges to a dressmaker's dummy beside the vast, brass till, like the headless, limbless ghost of its former proprietor. It reminded me of something in a museum, the kind that recreates historic high streets from bygone eras. Attractive in its way, but not somewhere you'd choose to live.

'It looks to me as if the shop's stock is all still inside,' I continued. 'Shouldn't Nell Little's executors have disposed of it all by now?'

I stood aside and beckoned Miles to peer through my makeshift porthole.

'Ah, yes, you're right. I remember now. Sadly, the departure of the old lady who used to run this delightful cottagecore outlet was what you might call unplanned. Poor soul never had the chance to dispose of the property in an organised manner. She probably hadn't heard of Swedish Death Cleaning.'

I flinched. I hadn't either, but it sounded a bit drastic for my liking.

So, Nell Little had died. I just hoped she didn't meet her end in the house. I had no desire to take on a ghost as a sitting tenant.

'But the good news is that everything inside is included in the asking price,' Miles added, his voice bright and cheery. 'That means you can either keep her stuff or sell it on at a profit.'

He probably hadn't lived long enough to accumulate as much clutter as Nell Little had, nor indeed as much as Steven, a compulsive collector.

'My girlfriend sells a load of her old stuff on Vinted.'

Most likely Barbie dolls and Sylvanian Families if she was the same age as him.

'It's a website for selling your unwanted, pre-loved clothes and bags and jewellery and shoes,' he added.

I bridled. He was a bit young for mansplaining.

I glanced at my watch, impatient to see inside now. Beyond the disused shop area, I might find some pleasant surprises. This looked like the kind of place that might have kept its original features. The light-filled shop area would make a very pleasant sitting room, using the wall-mounted shelves as bookcases. I could move the wooden counter into the kitchen to use as an island. Wasn't every kitchen meant to have an island these days? I wasn't the dinosaur Miles took me for.

'Vinted might provide a nice extra source of income besides your pension,' Miles was saying.

I gritted my teeth so hard that when I replied, I felt like a ventriloquist. Perhaps I could throw my voice to the dressmaker's dummy.

'I'm not retiring. I've at least another sixteen years to work before I can draw my state pension. Until then, I've got a good steady job at the city museum.'

Unperturbed, he gave me a radiant smile. 'Then it might be a lucrative hobby. My girlfriend says, pre-loved is the new new.'

Pre-loved? A bit like me, I thought, but didn't say. Once loved, an now discarded. Not that I'd fetch much of a price on Vinted, the way I was feeling.

He fumbled with a huge collection of keys attached on a chain to his belt loop. The weight of them made his trousers sag a little on one side, allowing his shirt tail to make a bid for freedom. This added to my impression that his suit had been bought to grow into, his first school uniform on going up to big school.

'So, are you ready to look inside now?' he was saying.

'As ready as I'll ever be,' I replied, and I followed him through the shop door.

* * *

His guided tour of the tumbledown cottage didn't take long. In the days before it had been converted into a shop, the room at the front would likely have been a neat and tidy parlour, reserved for Sundays and visitors. Behind lay a smaller room, once a kitchen, but now a dining room with a couple of low easy chairs in the corners. A single-storey, mid-century extension behind it housed a galley kitchen, smaller than the one I was used to, but ample for my needs. The vintage electric cooker would need a safety check, and the low, white, stone sink could have done with some bleach, but if it was cottagecore I was after, this would be a good starting point.

Double doors opened from the rear wall of the kitchen extension onto a long back garden the width of the house. Kicking the base of the damp doorframe to force it open, Miles led us out onto a semi-circle of Cotswold stone that the estate agent's particulars had described as a rustic terrace. Beyond lay a small, scraggy lawn, bordered by blossoming apple and lilac trees and flowering shrubs. What looked like an overgrown allotment beyond had presumably once been Nell Little's kitchen garden.

'Look, it's been rewilded,' exclaimed Miles, kicking aside a mesh of ivy creeping across the stepping stones, its stem swollen to the girth of a young tree trunk. 'Very good for the environment and low maintenance too. Ideal for anyone troubled by arthritis or similar.' He looked me up and down, as if checking for the frailties of old age. 'I expect your cat will enjoy exploring here,' he added.

'Just call me Schrödinger,' I murmured, turning my back on him and crossing the garden to the fence that ran the length of the right boundary. In the adjacent field, a couple of grazing donkeys came lolloping over to befriend me.

'You'd never get this much garden for the price in the city centre,' Miles called after me.

At least that was one thing we could agree on.

After a few minutes of stroking the donkeys' soft muzzles, I went to explore the rest of the plot. I trod carefully through the undergrowth in the old vegetable patch, looking out for fox droppings or worse. To my delight, beyond the dilapidated drystone wall at the bottom of the garden lay nothing but fields, where thick, green wheat was rippling in the warm breeze. That meant no human neighbours on two sides of the property. Such privacy would be a boon after living in the centre of town. On the third side lay a larger, old, stone house, with a massive drystone wall about eight feet high. My garden felt so secluded that it would feel like my own country estate.

Picturing myself spending summer evenings and weekends turning this quaint, unspoiled plot – unspoiled! I was starting to think like an estate agent myself now – into my own rural idyll, wandered back up the path towards Miles. He was ignoring the donkeys, who were lingering near to my fence, their heads close together as if in conversation as they swung their tails. Instead Miles was swotting up on his tablet. As I approached, the donkeys turned their soulful, brown eyes on me, and my heart melted.

plucked a handful of succulent dandelion leaves from my so-called lawn and dangled them over the fence.

'Here you go, my lovelies,' I crooned, waggling the leaves to encourage them. They didn't need to be asked twice, nibbling the proffered greenery without touching my fingers.

Miles picked up on my enthusiasm.

'Aren't they gorgeous?' he cooed. 'What could be more relaxing than coming home from work each evening to find these beauties waiting to greet you?'

It was an enticing image. To be honest, I knew I was being played, and I should have asked more questions, but he was telling me what I wanted to hear. Mostly.

'Provided your cat doesn't mind,' he added. 'Now, let's go and see the upstairs.'

* * *

The layout upstairs was predictable – the same as downstairs, minus the kitchen extension. The main bedroom was at the front, above the shop, and the second bedroom was over the dining room. A small section had been hived off from the smaller bedroom to form a compact bathroom as an afterthought. The cottage must have been built in the days of outdoor privies and tin baths in front of the fire.

Without the detritus of the shop's stock, the front bedroom felt much larger than the shop, even though it was fully furnished. I could picture the back bedroom, with its pleasant view of the garden, doubling as a dressing room – something I'd always fancied. But first, I'd have to jettison Nell Little's furniture. I already had a houseful of my own. Alternatively, as that had been bought jointly with Steven, and would always in my mind be associated with him, I could sell all that and have a completely fresh start.

Beneath the dust and cobwebs, Nell Little's furniture was solid wood and would polish up a treat, or I could give it an artsy makeover with trendy chalk paint.

I found it harder to warm to the bathroom – a clinical black-and-white-tiled affair with a dusty bath teeming with woodlice.

'A timeless monochrome,' enthused Miles. 'Easy to enliven with a pop of colour here and there.'

Honestly, I thought, *you should go on* Mastermind – *special subject: the euphemism.*

He pointed at the chequered floor.

'Do you like chess? You could make it a chess-themed bathroom.'

I shook my head. I wasn't going to tell him that Steven collected chess sets, amongst other things. That would only encourage him. Besides, I wasn't going to take style tips from someone whose suit didn't fit him properly.

As Miles began to descend the stairs, I ran a fingertip over the blistered varnish on the bannisters, sending conker-coloured flakes fluttering onto the threadbare stair carpet.

'So, now you've seen all of this delightful property, do you have any questions?' he asked when I caught up with him in the shop.

What had I forgotten?

'Ooh, parking. Is there rear access to the garden? I'd like to be able to park my car off-road.'

'Ve-hic-u-lar ac-cess?' He left a gap between every syllable that made me think he'd been practising that phrase. 'Not that I know of. But that doesn't mean there isn't any.' I admired his optimism. 'But you could always park on the hardstanding in front of the house. It's amply proportioned for a family car.'

Gazing out of the shop window with narrowed eyes, I decided my Fiat Panda would fit there with room to spare.

Suddenly, Taylor Swift began to sing, her voice – Miles's ringtone – muffled by his copious suit. He pulled his mobile out of his pocket and trotted back to the kitchen to take the call out of my earshot. Apparently, it didn't occur to him that the house was so small, I could still hear every word.

'Yes, she's definitely making buying signals,' I heard him say. To my surprise, I realised he was right.

As I waited for him to finish his call and return, I was already beginning in my head to design my change of address card for Curiosity Cottage. It was the first aspect of my forced relocation that I'd have total control over. That was a pleasingly empowering thought.

3

DIVIDE AND CONQUER

It was exactly the sort of cottage Steven would have hated. As soon as I got home, I clicked *send* on my email confirming my offer of five grand below the asking price, trusting to fate. If Swansong and Sons accepted my bid, the cottage was meant to be mine. If they haggled or told me other buyers were outbidding me, I'd let it go. Just because I was a cash buyer didn't mean I was prepared to get enmeshed in the gazumping shenanigans that had crept back into the property market lately. Whatever else Steven had taken from me, I still had my principles and my pride.

I also had my independence – a gift Steven inadvertently bestowed upon me when he announced he was leaving to find himself in India. With hindsight, it was a damning indictment of how far apart we'd drifted. I hadn't even realised he was lost.

After spending over half my life as part of a couple, I was now free to please myself at last. This included having the freedom to live wherever I liked that was within my budget. I could afford either an on-trend city-centre apartment, a small, new-build house on one of the many estates springing up in edge-of-town brownfield sites, or, as Miles Swansong had now persuaded me, a rambling cottage in the country.

Steven, I knew, would have gone for the smart city-centre apartment if he'd been staying in the UK. The very thought of rural living was enough to trigger his hay fever.

'I couldn't stand the farming smells or getting stuck behind a tractor on the way to work,' he objected when, around the tenth anniversary of our first date (we'd never married), I mooted we move to the country.

This was the man who thought nothing of inhaling exhaust fumes as he weaved his motorbike through city traffic jams morning and evening.

'They're notoriously stuck-up in those little villages,' he objected a few years later when he found me glued to an episode of *Escape to the Country*, my secret television vice. 'It takes generations to be accepted in a place like that. You'd always be an incomer.'

As he couldn't name any neighbours in our city centre street, that was hardly relevant, but his objections made me feel as if my dream of rural community life was completely beyond my reach.

However, as the years went by, we talked less and less about future plans, conversing only about the here and now, such as which film to watch on Netflix or which takeaway to order. Our regular date nights, which I instigated to try to rebuild our old closeness, were in cinemas or theatres – places in which it was impossible to talk to each other without being shushed by those around us. We might as well have fixed a date in his 'n' hers isolation tanks.

We lived in the moment, which for a while I thought was a good idea. Every newspaper or magazine I opened seemed to have an article on mindfulness, positing that focusing on the present was beneficial for mental health. Then I realised we were only living that way because neither of us was looking forward to a future together.

Even so, when I was about to hit fifty, I suggested that for practical reasons we should marry, or at least embark on a civil partnership. That way, whoever died first, the other would be able to remain in our house. As Steven was a lawyer, I thought he'd be keen on this idea, but when he declined, I decided he was just not ready yet to countenance his own mortality. Besides, my mum had drummed into me from when I was a teenager that boys mature later than girls. I gave Steven the benefit of the doubt. After all, he was eight months younger than me. It wouldn't be that long to wait for him to catch up. Don't we always believe what we want to believe?

Then, on the auspicious date of 1 April, a month after we'd celebrated paying the final instalment on our mortgage, I arrived back from work early one day to find him *in flagrante delicto*. No, not in bed with another woman, but in deep conversation with an estate agent, soliciting an evaluation on our beautiful Edwardian villa.

As I opened the front door, a woman in a tailored blazer and column dress was saying in clear, ringing tones, 'So your half, after the costs of sale, should amount to just short of four hundred grand.'

As soon as I flung the door open, they jumped apart, and Steven took an extra step backwards, a guilty grimace on his face. Even his quick wit as a lawyer couldn't help him come up with an innocent explanation for what I'd just heard.

Realising that she'd made a faux pas, the woman dropped her smartphone, which landed face up on the hall carpet, revealing the sum she'd just done on her calculator app. Despite my outrage, I couldn't help feeling sorry for her being such a dimwit as to need electronic help to divide eight hundred grand by two. But I focused the rest of my emotions – horror, wrath, indignation

– on Steven. By some miracle of self-control, I kept my voice low and calm.

'So, when were you going to tell me that you're planning to sell the house and leave me?'

That was the only reason she could be splitting the property's value in half.

Steven folded his arms across his chest.

'Don't make this all my fault,' he began, but the flustered estate agent interrupted.

'I think I'd better be going.'

'Oh no, please don't end your secret liaison on my account,' I retorted. 'I've better things to do. Like go and find a more competent estate agent to find a new forever home for myself.' I turned to Steven. 'And wherever you're going, you can take all your crap with you. My new place is going to be clean, tidy, minimalist and modern – not choc-a-bloc with your mad collections, you, you – you trainspotter, you!'

I apologise to trainspotters everywhere for that outburst, but I wasn't thinking rationally.

Steven cleared his throat. 'Actually, that's sort of the point. I'm going to put it all into storage and leave it behind until I have time to sell it. Or you can sell it for me, if you like, on commission. I want a fresh start, and I'll be taking only the essentials with me. On the road, I'll be living a minimalist life, unfettered by material possessions.'

He waved a hand at the clutter that filled every room in the house. In the entrance hall alone was his collection of curious walking sticks, five pairs of biker boots (who needs five pairs of biker boots when they have only two feet and one motorbike?), and a Shaker peg rail incongruously displaying baseball caps that looked ludicrous on a man no longer fit enough to play baseball.

'What minimalist hires a self-storage facility?' I snapped.

He ignored my jibe, perhaps because he knew he was being hypocritical. 'I plan to liquidate the rest of my assets to fund my travels for the rest of my life.'

'I'll liquidate your—'

'I'm sorry, I really think I should be going now,' said the estate agent, picking up her phone and striding to the front door in one smooth movement. 'Shall I send through the draft particulars in the morning, Mr Harris?'

Steven and I held each other's gaze for what seemed like an eternity, tears filling our eyes.

'Yes, please,' we both said at once, and that was the last thing we'd ever agreed on.

* * *

Despite the ignominious end of our relationship, I was determined not to allow myself to be fazed by any of Steven's requests. He'd made his decision, and I just wanted to move on and start over.

Steven was also in a hurry to be off. That same day, he began packing up all his belongings that wouldn't fit into his motorbike panniers, ready to remove them to a self-storage warehouse on the city outskirts, where he'd already booked a space. I didn't ask how much his monthly storage costs would be, but I was sure they were eye-watering.

'All I really need is to get the cash from my half of the house sale, and then I can be on my way,' he insisted.

And all I want is the half of my life that you took from me, I thought, but I didn't say it aloud, wanting to be the bigger person. Being combative wouldn't solve anything.

'What about working out your notice?' I asked, the morning after the estate agent's visit.

The last time he'd changed jobs, his contract had included a six-month notice period. At the time, he'd considered it a badge of honour, denoting his new employer thought him indispensable.

He closed his eyes, his face contorting with embarrassment. I guessed the truth before he could bring himself to tell me.

'Oh no, you've been sacked, haven't you? Is that what this is all about? You're worried you won't be able to get another job, so you've decided to do a runner instead.' My eyes widened in horror. 'Don't tell me you've done something illegal and must now flee the country to escape justice!'

I couldn't think what that might be. His work at a trademark lawyer was hardly high-risk.

When at last he spoke, his voice was barely audible.

'They paid me off in lieu of notice six months ago. I'm not being as impulsive as you think. I've had six months to think through my position and plan what to do with the rest of my life. This is definitely what I need and want to do. I'm sorry, Alice.'

Despite the harsh words that had passed between us, he put his arms around my neck and drew me close. I leaned into him, and we both wept, mourning the end of our non-marriage.

When I told my mum on the phone that night – it was the first time in weeks that I'd called her – she just tutted.

'Bit old to take a gap year, isn't he?'

Perhaps that was the problem. We hadn't allowed ourselves any freedom after graduation, just bowing to parental hopes to climb aboard the train of middle-class materialism. Only now had Steven engaged the ejector seat. But where did that leave me?

* * *

At work the next day, during my morning coffee break in the museum café, I made myself count my blessings. Once the house was sold, I'd have enough to buy at least a flat to live in mortgage-free. I had a job I enjoyed, and although my salary was much less than Steven's, it was enough for my modest needs. Now I'd also have complete control over my own space, which had been gradually eroded by Steven's clutter. Working in a museum had probably made me more sympathetic to his collections than most people, until they got out of hand. If I'd resisted earlier, would we have stayed together? Probably not. I couldn't blame his material goods for the breakdown in our relationship. It didn't mean I had to like them, though.

Positive thinking about my new, streamlined home enabled me to put on a brave face about Steven's departure. Emptied of his stuff, our house seemed twice its previous size, which no doubt helped speed up its sale. Our 'highly desirable residence', as the estate agent's blurb put it, with great access to local schools, shops and public transport links, was quickly snapped up by a professional couple with literally the classic two-point-four children. The wife was three and a half months pregnant, she proudly told us on their first viewing.

This made the sale especially poignant, because Steven and I had never been lucky enough to have children – or rather, we left it too late to try. Every time I asked him about it, he'd say, 'Ask me again when I'm forty,' and when that time came, it was too late. After a couple of years of trying, my body decided to go into early menopause. Looking back, I can't believe I went along with him to keep the peace. Although I bottled up my anger and disappointment, that was probably another reason why we eventually drifted apart.

On the day of Steven's departure, just before the sale was completed, I made him his favourite sandwiches (ham and coleslaw on granary) before waving him off on what must have felt to him like the first step towards the rest of his life. Mine too, I suppose.

When he turned the corner at the end of our road, disappearing from my view, I felt like half a person. Then, after staring for a moment at the *Sold* sign beside the front gate, I went back inside the house to start packing my own possessions, silently reciting that list of blessings like a Catholic telling a rosary.

If I'd known how many of those supposed blessings were about to be swept away, I'd probably have slumped on the stairs and wept. Instead, as I made up the first cardboard packing case, transforming it from flatpack to cube, my whole body began to tingle with a heady blend of liberation, excitement and trepidation. No more compromise! No more clutter! My future was all mine. Like the Doctor in *Doctor Who*, I would regenerate, and I couldn't wait to see how the new me would turn out.

4

THE DISAPPEARING DONKEYS

Danny Kimani, my best friend at work, set down two mugs of instant coffee on the table in the staff lunchroom.

'They're the least chipped mugs I could find,' he said. 'Honestly, you'd think the museum could run to some new ones now and again, even if they're only remaindered stock from the gift shop.'

I wrapped my hands around the mug and blew away the steam before taking a sip. Danny and I had just given a talk in the Victorian schoolroom to a noisy group of Year 5 visitors, and we needed to revive our voices before we took our turn on the welcome desk.

Actually, I'd borne the brunt of the session, as I was the museum's Victorian specialist. Danny's expertise is in classical civilisation, the subject of his degree. We learned a lot by doubling up on school talks, listening to each other bang on.

Now that my offer on the Cotswold Curiosity Shop had been accepted, I was bursting to tell him all about it. Previously, I hadn't allowed myself to get too excited in case it all fell through.

'My new house has got donkeys, Danny!'

'What, living in it? You're taking on four-legged lodgers?'

'No, silly. I don't mean they come with my new cottage. The

live next door. Well, in the field next to my new cottage, anyway. There isn't a house there, just an ancient stable in the far corner. Otherwise, it's just a paddock. I think they'll be the perfect neighbours.'

Danny raised his eyebrows. 'So, you won't have to worry about keeping up with the Joneses, even if the place does need a bit of a facelift.'

'Ha! Considering how ramshackle their stable is, what my cottage needs is like a touch of Botox compared to going under the knife.'

'Are you drawing on personal experience there?' he teased me.

I prodded his muscular calf with the toe of my trainer to reprimand him. He could take it.

'I know I've let myself go a bit since my split with Steven, but I'm not ready to resort to any kind of cosmetic surgery, thank you very much.'

I ran my fingers through my straggly hair, in dire need of at least a trim.

As Danny leaned back in his chair, he clasped his hands at the back of his head, pressing down his tight, black curls. He was only a few years younger than me, but as yet he didn't have a single grey.

'You do know donkeys are famed for their stubbornness,' he said. 'That's probably why you've hit it off with them.'

'Not these sweeties. I literally had them eating out of my hand the minute I met them. Can you imagine how soothing it'll be to go home to a pair of lovely donkeys each night after work? Especially after a day like today, trying to control thirty over-excited kids who treat us like clueless supply teachers. Just to see the donkeys' dear little faces—'

'Quite big faces, actually.'

'OK, dear big faces. But they're still cute. I'm kicking myself now for not taking their photos to show you. Anyway, I need have no worries about my new neighbours, at least on that side of the property.'

As I spoke, I recalled the high wall on the other side of my garden. I hadn't thought to ask Miles who lived behind it. For all I knew, I could be moving in next door to a serial killer, who built the wall so no-one couldn't see him burying dead bodies under his patio.

Danny pulled his phone out of his back trouser pocket. 'That's good to hear. I can't wait to see it for myself. I know you've already shown me the estate agent's blurb, but I'd like to get acquainted with the facts, not the fiction. Have you looked it up on Google Maps street view yet?'

I shook my head.

'What's its postcode?' he asked.

I'd had to write the address on so many forms as I prepared to move in – utilities, internet, mail forwarding, and so on – that I was able to recite the postcode from memory. The rest of the address sounded adorably picturesque: Curiosity Cottage, High Street, Little Pride, Gloucestershire.

Danny tapped the postcode into the Maps app on his phone, then spread two broad fingers to enlarge the aerial view of my future home. His brow furrowed as he held the screen up to show me.

'I see no donkeys.'

'I expect they're in their stable,' I replied, tapping the shed in the far corner of the paddock. 'See, there's a stable at the far corner of the field. Besides, it's not as if Google Maps is a livestream. I don't suppose the donkeys will be there all the time. They probably leave their field now and again.'

'Maybe their owner has a donkey-cart instead of a car. Maybe they were out pulling that about the village when the picture was taken.'

'Danny, I'm moving to the country, not travelling back in time,' I retorted. 'The invention of the combustion engine hasn't passed Little Pride by.'

'Well, how about tourists then? Tourists might like donkey rides. Perhaps their owner hires them out in the summer season. You can book traditional Mr Toad-style caravans for holidays these days. Something has to pull them. Why not your donkeys? Or maybe they've gone on a working holiday.'

'What, you mean they're now a double-act on a cruise ship? I don't think so.'

'I was thinking more of working on Weston-super-Mare beach for the summer season.'

That wasn't an unreasonable suggestion for late May.

I really wanted to believe him. 'I suppose you might be right.'

'It's been known to happen,' said Danny, affably.

I brightened. 'I wonder whether they're also hired out for nativity plays at Christmas and Palm Sunday processions at Easter? I hadn't thought of donkeys as a business proposition before. I thought people just kept them because they're nice. Everybody loves donkeys.'

'What a busy life your furry friends might lead.' There was a mischievous twinkle in his dark eyes. 'You're going to have so much to talk about together once you've moved in.'

'Which reminds me, I need to book Monday 20 June off to move house. Can you cover for me please while I nip up to Glen's office and get his approval before I put it on the chart?'

Glen, the museum's general manager, was a notoriously unsympathetic boss. I wasn't looking forward to his inevitable questions about why I was moving. I hadn't told him about the situation with Steven, although he might have picked it up on the grapevine.

'Sure. I doubt he'll object. I don't think anyone else is away until July or August. They're all saving their leave for the school holidays to fit around their kids. Besides, you've not had any time off at all yet this holiday year, have you?'

'True.'

Steven and I hadn't got round to planning so much as a mini break. When he'd seemed unwilling to commit to a specific time, I'd put that down to pressure of work at his busy office. I hadn't guessed it was because he was already planning to spend the rest of his life on holiday.

When I picked up my mug to put it in the dishwasher, the handle fell off. As I dropped both pieces in the bin, the unreliable, antique grandfather clock in the grand entrance hall struck half past three, indicating it was actually two o'clock. Danny and I parted in the corridor, Danny heading downstairs towards the welcome desk, while I dawdled up the stairs, rehearsing in my head what I'd say to Glen. His eyrie was on the top floor, away from where he might risk meeting actual museum visitors, the people who paid his (and my) wages. As I knocked on his door, I wondered whether I'd been foolhardy to book the removal van for my chosen date without first securing time off. But surely, in the circumstances, Glen couldn't say no?

5

THWARTED

'Glen said no!' I wailed to Danny, oblivious to the group of elderly people just starting their guided tour with our colleague Myrtle.

'What?' In his vicarious frustration, Danny thumped his mouse down on the ripped mouse mat, and its little wheel fell off.

'Poor mouse,' I said. 'Now it looks how I feel.'

I picked up the mouse and laid it gently on its back, ready to perform emergency surgery with the paperknife. I'd had to do this three times in the last fortnight, my requisition for a new mouse having gone unheeded. Lately, it was starting to feel as if the whole museum was held together only by paperclips and rubber bands.

'On what grounds did Glen refuse?' asked Danny, watching me twiddle the tiny screw with my fingernail to get the back off the mouse.

'He said no leave is allowed that day unless someone dies, because at 4 p.m. the whole museum will close for a special staff meeting. He wouldn't tell me what for, though.'

I unhooked the tiny spindle inside the mouse and threaded the wheel back on.

'That would be an extreme way to wangle a day off,' said Danny. 'I hope you're not thinking of bumping anyone off?'

'Don't tempt me!' I grimaced, remembering Glen's smug smile as he turned down my request. He knew he held all the power, and he made the most of it.

'Maybe we're going to have a special visitor, like a member of the royal family,' Danny speculated. 'That would explain the early closing. They won't want the hoi-polloi of the general public cluttering up the place. Glen will want to invite special guests, ones he can count on to be washed and freshly pressed, and who won't try to pinch the exhibits or punch each other while they think we're not looking.'

Both of those things had happened with our Year 5 party earlier.

I gave a half-hearted smile. Danny always tried to cheer me up when I was down.

'No, if that was the case, maintenance would be scurrying about just now touching up chipped paintwork and removing frayed carpets.'

Danny grinned fondly at me. 'Like I always say, Alice, you've missed your vocation. Ever the museum detective.'

'And cleaner and washer-upper and IT repairman.' I waved the mouse. 'Let alone what's actually on my job description.'

I replaced the back of the mouse and dropped it into Danny's outstretched hand. 'Here you go. Give your little robo-rodent friend a test drive. Anyway, it looks as if I'll have to do all my moving over the previous weekend now instead. I don't suppose—'

Danny, usually so supportive, put up his free hand in self-defence. 'Sorry, no can do. Martin's just booked a special mini break that weekend. Don't know where, but I think it's somewhere fancy and he's paying.'

As deputy director, Danny's boyfriend earned much more than our grade.

'Really? You don't think he's planning a proposal, do you?'

'A proposal?' Danny shrieked.

I guessed he wasn't as serious about their relationship as Martin was, even though he'd recently moved into Martin's apartment. As his best friend, I should have been happy for him, but there was something about Martin that I couldn't warm to.

The visitors turned as one to stare at us. Danny turned to apologise.

'Sorry to have startled you, ladies and gentlemen, there's no cause for alarm.'

Myrtle, the museum's artistic director, who knew all about Danny's relationship with Martin, decided to brighten up her dreary tour with a spot of mischief.

'So, you proposed to Danny at last, Alice? I'm sure our visitors will join me in wishing you every happiness together. You make a lovely couple.'

Then she led the tour group in a round of applause.

Trying not to laugh, Danny played along, offering a gracious thank you and drawing me to his broad chest in a hug. I buried my face in his ample shoulder, shaking with a mix of indignation and laughter, until Danny assured me they'd moved out of earshot to the local geology section. I wriggled free and dusted myself down.

'At least your recent crisis hasn't quashed your sense of humour,' he assured me. 'Anyway, where were we? Oh yes, what other reason could there be to close the museum early on your moving day?'

'A staff party to thank us for soldiering on while the museum falls apart around us? The announcement of a major investment plan to stop any more bits dropping off? Glen announcing his retirement?'

'Any of those would be fine by me,' said Danny. 'Either way, I think an office sweepstake is in order.'

Danny never missed an opportunity for an office sweepstake.

'Speaking of missed vocations, Danny, you'd have made a great bookie,' I replied.

For the rest of our stint on the welcome desk, Danny and I dreamed up dozens of different reasons for the mysterious meeting, and we wrote them on little slips of paper to dish out to our colleagues next day.

As I drove home after work, I was still trying to second-guess the real reason for the mysterious meeting. I hoped my reputation as the museum's sleuth wouldn't let me down.

6

CURBED ENTHUSIASM

I was vaguely conscious that it was Midsummer's Day when a knock at the door broke so violently into my sleep that I thought for a moment my unexpected visitor was pounding at it with a hammer or even a pickaxe.

Why hadn't the postman or whoever it was used our beautiful brass knocker in the shape of a dolphin – one of five in Steven's collection – or the Edwardian bellpull that he had recently restored to full working order?

With my eyes still closed, I heaved myself up into a sitting position and swung my legs over the side of the bed, feeling around with my bare toes for my slippers. Instead of my soft, fluffy bootees, they struck something cold and hard – the edge of the suitcase containing all my nightclothes, except the gingham pyjamas that I had on.

Despite the pounding in my head, I opened my eyes, expecting shutter-induced darkness. Steven and I had trendy, Colonial-style shutters fitted the previous year. At once, I squeezed them tight shut against the brilliant sunshine that had been pouring in my bedroom window since about four o'clock in the morning.

Assuming I'd literally got out of the wrong side of bed that morning, I squinted around the room to get my bearings. Nothing else was where it should be either.

Then I remembered. That house was history. I'd moved into my new cottage on Saturday, and this was Tuesday. That meant it was the morning after the museum's mysterious early closing day for which Glen had refused me leave.

In the office sweepstake, I'd picked the least likely reason: alien invasion. My disappointment was nothing compared to my distress when I discovered the real reason for the meeting: an immediate drastic reduction in staffing, achieved through redundancies, myself included.

Priority was given to keeping workers who had family responsibilities or who were towards the start of their careers. The older, single workers like me were to be made redundant, regardless of how long we'd served there. The only exception was Danny, a few years younger than me, who was allowed to keep his job. It was pretty obvious his relationship with Martin had spared him the axe.

I was astonished. Surely this approach would cost the museum much more in redundancy payouts than a last-in, first-out strategy. Then I realised the youngsters were on lower salaries, therefore cheaper to retain.

'Surely this can't be legal,' I cried, as soon as Glen had delivered the lethal blow. Where was my live-in lawyer when I needed him? Probably halfway to India by now. 'I've been here for donkeys years. Shouldn't loyalty be reciprocated? Besides, living alone is more expensive than being in a partnership. It's like there's a tax on being single. Why should those living with partners get preferential treatment?'

'Alice, you're jumping to false conclusions,' Glen replied in the brusque tone of a schoolteacher reprimanding a lippy pupil. 'We've been as generous as we can in the circumstances, and far more even-handed than you give us credit for. You, for example, are mort-gage-free and are assured of rent-free housing for life. Others here are under much greater financial constraints, whether or not they live with a partner.'

'Yes, but I'm only mortgage-free because I've worked very hard ever since I graduated,' I retorted. 'I never even took time out for maternity leave.' It hurt me to say that, but I was prepared to use all the ammunition at my disposal to save my job. 'So, now I'm being penalised for thirty years' uninterrupted service?'

Glen didn't reply, instead calling on someone with their hand up to put their question. Danny, sitting next to me, slipped his arm around my shoulders, and I slumped against him. After the week-end's upheaval of moving house, even with the removal men doing the heavy lifting, I didn't have the strength to fight any further, especially when it seemed a hopeless case.

To be truthful, Glen's remarks made sense to me. Although I wasn't about to admit it, if I'd had to choose between myself and Jenna, a single parent who worked full-time in the gift shop to support two children in a council flat, I'd have kept her on instead of me.

Staring at the leaflet Glen had just passed to all the redundant staff, I did a quick mental calculation of how much my redundancy package would be worth. At least that was a pleasant surprise: three months' pay.

I tried to look on the bright side. I'd have plenty of time to unpack and settle into my new home. My unclaimed holiday would cancel out my notice period. That would give me a generous amount of time in which I could afford not to earn any money. Or I could get a new job as soon as I could, leaving me with useful rainy-day money in the bank. So where would I start?

A volley of rapid knocks brought me back to the present.

Oh yes, by answering the door.

Checking my pyjamas hadn't come adrift in the night, I stumbled down the stairs into the front room. A frisson of fear ran through me as I detected a low, rumbling sound coming from the sofa. Had the hammerer got weary of waiting for me, smashed his way in, then nodded off? Surely I hadn't taken that long to descend the stairs?

The sofa faced away from me towards the fireplace, and I couldn't see who was lying there. It clearly wasn't the hammerer, as the bashing was starting up again. Figuring another minute would make no odds at this stage, I tiptoed across to the sofa and peered over the back to identify the phantom snorer.

Danny! His sturdy limbs were squeezed onto the compact two-seater sofa like sardines in a can, and the patchwork quilt he must have fetched from the old shop in lieu of proper bedding had slipped off his broad torso, pooling in a heap on the floor.

What on earth was Danny doing there? I glanced at my watch. And at gone midday too. Come to that, why had I slept so late?

There seemed no urgency to wake him from his babylike slumber. I'd deal with him once I'd made us both some coffee and taken some painkillers for this headache that had come from nowhere.

A shrill cry came from outside the front door of the shop: 'I know you're in there!'

First, I needed to deal with my unexpected visitor. I wanted to find out who was treating my front door like a percussion instrument.

Running my hands quickly over my long, loose hair to flatten any bits sticking up, I went over to open the door at last. On the doorstep stood a little old lady, her face obscured in shadow against the bright sunshine behind her. She must have weighed about five stone, her meagre frame dwarfed by layers of thick handknits and a sagging, straight, tweed skirt that almost reached her ankles. She was wringing her tiny, bent hands across her chest. Surely such skinny fingers couldn't have made such a racket?

A glance at her feet told me all I needed to know. She was wearing hob-nailed, steel-capped workmen's boots several sizes too big for her, presumably her husband's or her son's. She raised her walking stick to shake at me.

'Have you seen what's on your front path?' she demanded.

When she raised her hands to her cheeks to project her horror, she looked like the older sister of *The Scream* by Edvard Munch.

I peered over her shoulder. 'You mean my car?'

It wasn't that bad for a ten-year-old vehicle. Surely she wasn't worried I was lowering the tone of the neighbourhood? It had barely a dent – although I didn't remember the huge scrape all down the passenger side. Considering how scruffy she looked, she was hardly in a position to call me out on that score, but her agitated manner was unnerving me.

I tried to sound calm. 'What do you think is wrong with my car exactly?'

'You didn't oughta of parked it like that there.' She jabbed a twisted thumb over her shoulder without removing her beady eyes from me.

I followed the direction of her thumb. OK, so I was parked a little wonky, but I wasn't yet used to reversing at right angles onto this narrow hardstanding. At my old house, I'd had to park on the street and was a wiz at parallel parking. I tried to reassure her.

'I'm sorry, I'm usually much better at parking. I don't know why I didn't park more neatly last night.'

I couldn't see why she was so worked up about it. What had it to do with her anyway?

'It oughta be the last time too.' She took a few steps back down the path and pointed to where the hardstanding met the road. 'No dropped kerb, see? You can't park your car where there's no dropped kerb. It ain't right. You can't just drive over the pavement. You might run down a helpless old person.'

Don't put ideas into my head, I thought. Although to be fair, she seemed far from helpless.

'You could run one of your customers right over, or some kiddies enjoying an ice cream. Then where would you be?'

I ran my hand over my eyes to block out the sunshine corkscrewing into my brain.

'What customers?' I replied. 'It's only me here now.'

As if to brand me a liar in front of my new neighbour, a loud groan and a yawn reverberated around the living room, followed by a creak of sofa springs and the soft thud of bare footsteps. Danny, having roused from his slumber, padded out to the front door to see what all the fuss was about.

At the sight of a tall, broad, black man in only his boxers, the old lady nearly fell over backwards.

'That's not what we call alone around here!' she shrieked, as she darted back to the pavement. She paused to point at her feet. 'No dropped kerb!' was her parting shot. Then she fled up the high street as fast as her outsized boots would carry her.

I had a sinking feeling she was off to regale the whole village with the details of her encounter, turning my new neighbours against me before they'd even met me and had a chance to get to know what I was really like.

I slammed the front door and turned to Danny.

'That went well,' I said sardonically as I followed him through to the kitchen.

'Don't worry, she's only one person,' said Danny. 'For all you know, everyone else in the village might think she's a mad old bat and pay no attention to what she says about you. Anyway, forget about her. A crazy lady on the doorstep is the least of your troubles after last night.'

'Last night?' I faltered. I was struggling to recall what had happened after the staff meeting. 'Why?'

Danny sank down onto a rickety, bentwood chair that had come with the house. I hoped it was strong enough to bear his weight.

'You mean you don't remember?'

I shook my head, which I at once regretted. I laid one hand on the edge of the little dining table to stop the room from spinning.

'Then you'd better sit down and let me make us a restorative cuppa before I remind you.'

As I slumped down onto the other bentwood chair, its leg fell off. This was not turning out to be the best of days.

7

WARNING BELLS

'I guess I'll have to apply to the council for planning permission for a dropped kerb so I can park my car there,' I said to Danny mournfully as he filled the teapot. 'Honestly, you'd think the estate agent would have told me about that. I wonder how long it will take for them to install it.'

Danny took two bone-china cups and saucers from the draining board and set them on the table.

'It doesn't much matter. You probably won't be needing it for at least a year after last night.'

'What do you mean?'

Danny avoided eye contact with me as he brought the teapot to the table. 'Because that's how long a driving ban you're likely to get if your blood test proves positive.'

I couldn't believe what I was hearing. 'Sorry, Danny, can you stop being mysterious and just tell me the worst? I don't remember doing anything wrong.'

Resting my elbows on the table, I cradled my aching head in my hands.

Danny poured some milk into the cups before pouring the tea and sliding one across the table to me.

'Do you remember anything about last night?'

I considered for a moment. 'No, not really, only that awful staff meeting. Oh, and arriving in the pub not long afterwards. And then Martin buying us drinks. I think Glen had given him money to stand us all a drink or two.'

'And what did you have to drink exactly?'

I frowned. Why was he being so judgemental?

'Only orange juice and lemonade, I promise, because I knew I was driving home.'

Besides which, I had no intention of adding a hangover to my misery.

Danny sat down opposite me, took a sip of his tea and cleared his throat. 'I thought so, or I'd have confiscated your car keys. By the way, if it makes you feel any better, it isn't your fault that your car's not parked straight.'

'Even so, it's odd. You know tidy parking is one of my superpowers, and that was just a ninety-degree reverse from the main road. I can do simple manoeuvres like that with my eyes closed.'

Danny shuddered. 'I wouldn't try that if I were you. Anyway, the reason it's wonky is because you didn't park it.'

I set my cup on its saucer. I had a funny feeling that what he was about to say might make me spill my tea.

'Then who did? Was it you?' That made sense. I had a vague recollection of crying on his shoulder in the pub. But that didn't explain why he'd parked my car. 'It was kind of you to see me home, but it wasn't necessary. You are the only other person that came home with me last night – aren't you?'

I strained my ears, listening for tell-tale sounds of a third party elsewhere in the house. Martin, maybe? I hoped not. Although I'd tried to be nice to Martin at work for Danny's sake, I didn't much like him.

But the rest of the house lay in silence.

'I know, but I wanted to talk to you alone about the whole business without any of the rest of the museum staff earwigging. But with all of them around us in the pub, there was no chance,' said Danny. 'You were pretty upset.'

'I'd have been fine on my own, honestly.'

'Maybe for the first part of the journey,' he replied slowly. 'But not after the traffic officer had stopped us.'

He paused, as if hoping that with enough clues I'd remember, sparing him the tricky task of telling me himself.

His ploy worked. His mention of the traffic officer triggered an action replay in my head, from the blue light flashing in my rear-view mirror as I hit the motorway, to the prick of the doctor's needle in the crook of my left elbow.

I buried my head in my hands and slumped forward.

'It's Glen's fault,' I mumbled into my hands. 'If he hadn't made me redundant, I wouldn't even have been in such a state. You know what a good driver I am.'

I pride myself on never having had any points on my licence, nor a single parking ticket.

I raised my head just enough to look him in the eye. I couldn't really blame Glen. My emotional reaction was my own responsibility. Then I had an idea.

'Maybe someone gave me the wrong drink. A gin and orange instead of an orange and lemonade.'

'I may be teetotal, but even I know that gin and orange isn't served by the pint,' he pointed out. 'Besides, you were among friends. It's not as if you were out clubbing, surrounded by strangers. Although to be honest, you didn't start behaving as if you were drunk until we were halfway back here. At first, your driving was as good as ever – much better than mine, as usual. Then you suddenly slowed right down and started swerving from one lane to another and talking incoherent nonsense. You frightened the life out of me. I thought you were having a stroke or something, because I knew you were sober as a nun. I was just going to tell you to pull over when the police car speeding up behind us saved me the trouble.'

'Oh no, the dreaded breathalyser! I remember it now. My first ever, and I hope it will be my last. It can't possibly have been positive.'

'You're right, it was negative. But for some unknown reason, your speech was slurred, and you almost fell to the ground when they asked you to step out of the car. So, they took you back to the station for a repeat breath test, and also a blood test, because they thought they might have had a faulty batch of breathalysers.'

'That accounts for this, then.' I clutched my arm where the needle had gone in. It was tender to the touch. When I ripped off the small sticking plaster, I discovered a small, mottled bruise with a dark-red dot at its centre.

'Surely the second breath test and the blood test would have cleared me? They must have been right about the faulty breathalysers.'

Danny nodded. 'I agree about the breathalysers. But as a matter of procedure, apparently they had to send the blood test away for analysis, although it seems like a massive waste of time and resources to me. They said you can still drive in the meantime, though, unless and until you have to go to court.'

I cringed.

'Go to court? Surely it won't come to that? Still, look on the bright side.' I gave a hollow laugh. 'At least I don't have to grovel to Glen to ask for time off to go to prison. My time is my own now.'

'Don't worry, Alice, I'm sure it won't come to a jail sentence, not with a negative breath test. As my mum always says, don't go to meet trouble halfway.'

I scrunched my eyes closed, vainly hoping to stop the tears in my eyes from spilling onto my cheeks.

'You can't know that for sure, Danny. If their breathalysers are faulty, their blood tests might be too. How will I get to work from here if I lose my driving licence? If anyone wants to employ a washed-out fifty-year-old, that is.'

Danny came over to put an arm around my shoulders and gave the top of my head a comforting kiss.

'Don't be daft. Plenty of people. You've loads to offer. You're just at a low ebb. You've had just about every stress factor going in the last few months: ending a long-term relationship, moving house, losing your job. But you're going to be fine, trust me. I know you. You'll bounce back one way or another.' He cast his arm about the room. 'For a start, you're going to make a lovely little home here, where you'll be so much happier than living among all Steven's crap.' Although Danny had a higher tolerance of clutter than I did, he only liked valuable antique clutter with an impressive provenance – not the sort of kitsch nonsense Steven collected. 'Besides, until you get the all-clear on the blood test, I'm sure you must be able to get a bus into town from here. The central bus station's always heaving with buses from all over. Just think of all the reading you can catch up with if you're commuting by bus rather than having to sit at the wheel in that dreadful stop-start traffic every morning and evening.'

I sniffed as I leaned into his hug. 'And I won't start and end each working day with a barrage of bad language at the traffic jams. There's no excuse for my behaviour last night though, Danny. I know I was pretty distraught at being made redundant, but that shouldn't have been enough to make me drive so badly. Oh God, I could have killed someone. I could have killed you. I'm so sorry.

And, by the way, do apologise to Martin for my having hijacked you for the night. I hope he didn't mind.'

I covered my face with my hands.

'Oh, don't worry about Martin. Just look after yourself for a change. And remember, things are going to get better from here on in, I promise you.'

I nodded, starting to rally a little. Then a missing piece of the jigsaw leaped into my head.

'So how did we get home last night? I presume the traffic officers weren't about to let me drive home from the police station if they honestly thought I was incapable. Surely they didn't chauffeur us home? Or was it a slow night, murder-wise, and they needed something to do?'

Danny hesitated. 'Actually, I drove us back here. Once they'd finished all their paperwork, they said they thought it best if your husband drove you home.'

I gasped. 'What, Steven? Where did he spring from? I thought he'd be in Istanbul by now.'

Danny grinned, pointing to himself. 'They meant me. But don't worry, we didn't secretly tie the knot while you were tipsy. We were in Broadwick, not Las Vegas.'

I burst out laughing. 'I could have done worse, but I'd hate to upset Martin.'

'Oh, for goodness' sake, stop fretting about Martin.'

I felt bad for not being fonder of Martin for Danny's sake. Still, he made Danny happy, and that was what mattered.

'I promise I'll never complain about your inept parking again,' I added, contrite.

Danny patted my shoulder in encouragement and returned to his seat.

'That's more like it. But I'm afraid there's one more bit of bad news.' He grimaced. 'Alice, I'm really sorry, but when I turned into the narrow lane that leads off the main road into the village, I misjudged the distance between the car and the drystone wall.'

After he'd been so kind, I could hardly tell him off.

'You mean you scraped it? No matter. It's only a bit of metal. I'm just thankful you got me home safely.'

'Actually, I wrecked the offside front light. I'm sorry to add to your woes, but it's going to need a replacement part. You must let me take it to the garage near Martin's flat – our flat – and get it fixed for you at my own expense,' he added. 'I insist.'

I shrugged. I could hardly object. He sat back in his chair, shoulders sagging in relief.

'That's sorted then. Now, why don't you go and have a shower and get dressed? Then the world will start to look a better place.'

I glanced at the clock. 'Oh my God, we're going to be so late for work. Glen will go bananas.'

Danny shook his head. 'Don't worry, I phoned Martin when we got back here last night and told him to tell Glen I was poorly today. And you don't have to go to work either. Don't you remember telling Glen after the meeting that you'd be taking your month's holiday owing in lieu of notice, with immediate effect?'

'Did I? Oh well, that's something. I don't think I could face anyone just yet after making such a fool of myself.'

Danny gave me a squeeze before getting to his feet. 'Don't worry, they'll understand. They know you've been having a rough time lately. Now, what's a man got to do around here to get some breakfast?'

I gave a watery smile. 'You've already done more than enough to earn yourself bacon and eggs.'

I heaved myself out of the chair, glad to have a task to focus on that would take my mind off the previous evening's events.

8

AT THE BUS STOP

'What do you mean, there's no village bus service?'

After Danny had departed in my car, I wandered up to the bus stop at the centre of the village to check out the timetable. A man in a hooped green rugby shirt and oxblood, corduroy trousers was loitering in the old-fashioned, brick-built bus shelter. For his age – mid-sixties, at a guess – he wouldn't have been bad looking if he pruned the bushy eyebrows that gave a clue to the colour his hair had been before he lost it. Once black, they were now streaked with white, like two baby badgers.

'You're new to the village, aren't you? Or are you just visiting?'

'I've just moved here,' I said, unsure how much to reveal to this stranger. Then I thought, *No, it's me who's the stranger in town – well, village, anyway.* I should have been more trusting. This little rural community would surely be safer than the city.

'Then I'm sorry to tell you our bus service was axed several years ago. The bus company couldn't make it pay.'

My shoulders drooping in defeat, I slumped onto the wooden slatted seat that spanned the bus shelter. 'Honestly, what is it with me lately? Everything I touch goes wrong.'

'Like a reverse Midas touch?'

'Exactly right. I've just sold my house in town and moved here on Saturday, only to lose my job two days after my move. I might also be about to lose my car.' I said 'car' rather than 'licence', so he didn't take me for a drunken or otherwise dangerous driver. 'Then today I find there's no local bus to take me to interviews, or to work, if and when I get another job.'

The man pulled a face that I think he meant to be sympathetic – a cross between a kindly smile and a frown, the corners of his wide mouth turning down while the rest of it curved upward. His dark eyes, olive skin and aquiline nose made me wonder if he had Mediterranean ancestry. What with his broad shoulders, thick arms and sturdy thighs, he put me in mind of an ancient Roman soldier.

Then I reined in my imagination. I wouldn't allow my newly single, isolated status to make me a pushover for the first stranger who was kind to me. I may have been feeling vulnerable, but I didn't need a man to make a success of my new life.

'But hang on,' I said, pulling myself together. 'If there's no bus service, why is there a bus shelter? And what are you waiting for if not a bus?'

He turned to tap the large noticeboard affixed to the back wall of the shelter, the old-fashioned kind that takes drawing pins. Two glass doors stood open, and a small gold key hung in the lock of the right-hand one.

'I've just been putting up this month's notices.' He closed the doors and turned the key, which he then extracted and slipped into his trouser pocket. 'Are you by any chance Alice Carroll? The lady who's just bought Nell Little's Cotswold Curiosity Shop?'

I blinked. How could he tell?

'Yes, I've bought the property,' I said tentatively, puzzled as to why he referred to it as Nell Little's shop when Nell Little was long gone.

He must have sensed my discomfort, because he set down the yellowing papers he'd just removed from the board and held his hand out for me to shake as a more formal welcome. His grip was strong and confident, and I returned it even more firmly to assert my strength of character.

'I'm Andrew Gloster, by the way, editor of the *Little Pride Parish News*.' He spelled out his surname for clarity. 'Not like Gloucester, the city.' He held up the papers he'd just taken down. 'One of my many duties is to post this handy checklist of village events and opening times on the parish noticeboard as each new issue is published. You'll have to let me know the new trading hours for the shop as soon as you're ready.' He tapped a spot on the list of opening times:

Nell Little's Curiosity Shop – temporarily closed pending change of proprietor.

'It'll be good to see a light in the shop window again. It's been bereft of life for too long after what happened to poor Nell Little.'

I rubbed my eyes. 'I'm sorry, I think there's been a misunderstanding. I've purchased the cottage to live in, not as a business. I'm planning to turn the shop area into a sitting room.'

His broad forehead furrowed, making the tiny badgers dive downwards together, like synchronised swimmers. 'But you must reopen the shop. It was sold as a going concern.'

Feeling the blood draining out of my face, I leaned back on the bench. The pebbledash on the rear wall of the bus shelter dug into my flesh through my thin cardigan.

When he sat down beside me at a respectful distance away, I realised there was no reason not to trust him. As editor of the parish magazine, he was presumably a decent, respected member of the community. I could be frank with him. He might even prove helpful.

'That's not what the estate agent told me. He knew I was after a house, not a business.'

'Then your solicitor has been rather remiss not to pick up his mistake.'

I appreciated his tact. If he was correct about the terms of sale, he must have been thinking I was an idiot, even if he was kind enough not to say so. 'Oh no, don't tell me you did your own conveyancing to save money?' He winced. 'I've seen people caught out that way before. Not hiring a professional is always a false economy.'

I held up my hand in protest. 'No, I'd never dream of doing that. I was lucky enough to have a – a close friend who's a lawyer, who kindly did the conveyancing for me.'

I didn't reveal that the friend was my ex. I didn't want to look like a complete victim. Actually, I was as much the victim of my own softness as of Steven's incompetence. I should never have let him handle the purchase, as he was quite the wrong kind of lawyer. I just felt sorry for him for losing his job, and I thought giving him one final legal task before he left would bolster his ego. What was I thinking?

'And this friend of yours, was she an experienced conveyancer?'

I didn't correct his use of the feminine pronoun.

'Not exactly.' I spoke slowly, choosing my words with care, as I'm a dreadful liar. 'But I thought they needed the work, and that using them would speed things up.'

Andrew sat back, his hands on his oxblood trousers, legs together. At least he wasn't manspreading while mansplaining.

'Then it's a pity your friend didn't repay your generosity by doing a proper job of it. I'm astonished she didn't explain that you are obliged to open the shop at least occasionally. You'll need to keep the front room permanently stocked and looking like a shop, unless and until you apply to the council for change of use from retail to residential.'

'Fine, I'll do that, then.' I laid a hand on my chest to calm my pounding heart. 'Goodness, Andrew, you frightened me there for a minute.'

Before speaking, he pressed his thin lips tightly together, making his mouth suddenly look mean. I realised I wouldn't like to get on the wrong side of him.

'It may not be that simple, Alice. The council's already turned down a change-of-use application for your cottage. They even rejected the builder's appeal, which is most unusual. You see, the council are currently campaigning to stop local shops from disappearing, and they wanted to make yours a case in point.'

'What, even a musty old bric-a-brac shop like mine?' Mine? What was I saying? I was no shopkeeper. 'If it sold daily essentials like milk and bread and newspapers, I could understand. But surely Nell Little's Cotswold Curiosity Shop was never essential to the village community. After all, you've done without in the year or so it's been closed.'

'Ah, but losing any local shops can kill a rural community. People stop going out and about on foot, and instead jump in the car to head for the nearest shopping mall or city centre. Money leaves the village rather than coming into it. We're always in pursuit of the foreign pound here.'

'Foreign? What, you mean the shop takes euros and dollars?'

He'd be telling me next that I needed to apply for a village passport.

He bit back a bemused smile. 'No, I mean we want to attract spending by people from beyond the parish.'

'How do you know all this exactly?' I queried, hoping he was passing on idle hearsay rather than hard fact.

'I get it straight from the horse's mouth – from the parish council. I go to public meetings of the parish and district councils for my reports in the *Parish News*. The magazine isn't just about diary dates. It also shares a monthly update on planning applications, including the verdicts of the district council and the parish council. The district council has the final say, and it doesn't always see what's best for the village. It's pretty town-centric. But I've lived in Little Pride all my life, apart from when I was at boarding school and university, and then on foreign postings, so I have my finger on the village pulse.'

Foreign postings? I pictured him wrapped up in brown paper like a giant parcel before realising he meant in some military or diplomatic capacity. If he'd had a glamorous life abroad, editing the *Little Pride Parish News* in his retirement must have seemed a comedown.

So distracted was I by this revelation that something he'd said earlier was only just registering.

'Hang on a minute. Builder? What builder? Why was a builder applying for a change of use for my cottage?'

I was surprised how proprietorial I was feeling already, but how dare some unknown builder muscle in on my territory?

'That was long before you bought it, when it first came on the market. Terence Bolt was after the cottage as a kind of traditional anchor for the new housing estate he's building next door to you.'

I froze. 'What new housing estate?'

'In the old paddock. Didn't you know about that either?' He tutted at my ignorance. 'When Bolt buys up bare plots of land like that, he tries to acquire at least one adjacent old building to add a touch of historic context for the new-builds. He's obliged by local planning regulations to echo the local vernacular, because Little Pride lies in an Area of Outstanding Natural Beauty. But in this case, the villagers campaigned against his scheme, led by you other next-door neighbour, Bob Sponge, because they're fond of the Cotswold Curiosity Shop and didn't want to lose it. Coupled with the district council's policy of keeping local shops open, he didn't have a prayer of getting his change-of-use application approved. Didn't stop him trying to buy the council off, though. He's a slippery one, is Terence Bolt.'

'Buy the council off?'

'Oh, yes,' replied Andrew. 'No one can prove it, but rumour has it' – he leaned closer to me and lowered his voice, as if fearing the bus shelter was bugged – 'that's how he got permission to build so many houses on the paddock in the first place. Technically, it's within the village building line, so it counts as infill, rather than being a greenfield site, despite literally being a field that's green. No one wanted to lose the paddock either. It's been animal grazing and stabling for as long as anyone can remember.'

'I don't want it built on either,' I replied. 'I was looking forward to having those beautiful donkeys as neighbours.'

I turned my head away from Andrew, hoping he wouldn't notice the tears of frustration welling up in my eyes. He glanced at his watch.

'Goodness knows, there are plenty of other donkeys in the village that you'll meet soon enough, including a couple on the parish council.'

I goggled at him. 'Really?'

He gave a low chuckle. 'Yes, but not the four-legged, furry kind. And here comes one of them.' He raised his hand to wave to the old lady in hobnailed boots, who was just marching down the high street from the village shop at an impressive speed for someone of her age. Underneath the baggy, tweed skirt, she must have had powerful legs, not least to keep her outsized, heavy footwear moving. If roused, she probably had a kick like a wild horse. I hoped she wouldn't recognise me, now that I was dressed and had brushed my hair, but she must have done, as she glared at me, shaking her fist. Andrew smirked as he lowered his voice.

'Don't mind old Maudie Frampton. She's not as dangerous as she looks, provided you keep on the right side of her. She's just averse to change, like a lot of people round here. Anyway, it's a pleasure to meet you, Alice, but now I must press on. Let me know when you've decided your new opening hours, so that I can include them in the next *Parish News*. If you pick up a copy from Suki's Stores, you'll find my contact details on the inside front page. Oh, and if you want to stage a special grand reopening event, give me a shout, and I'll throw in a free ad to get you off to a great start. Top tip, by the way – if you want to lure villagers along to any event, offer tea and cake. Not much happens around here without tea and cake.'

As he got to his feet, Andrew's encouraging smile revealed expensive-looking dentistry. When he held out his hand for me to shake again, his formality surprised me, but perhaps that was either the norm in his professional background, or just the local custom in Little Pride.

I wondered whether Bob Sponge would offer such a formal welcome. As to Terence Bolt, the only gesture I wanted to make to him right now was much less polite.

9

SUKI'S STORES

Before heading back to the cottage, I stopped off at the village shop opposite the bus stop to buy a copy of the *Little Pride Parish News*.

'Ah, you must be the new Nell,' was the greeting of an impossibly slender young woman behind the counter.

'My name's Alice Carroll,' I replied. 'Although I've just moved into Nell Little's former cottage, if that's what you mean.'

I held out my hand for her to shake. When she looked at me oddly, I assumed she was being stand-offish. Then I realised she might have been wondering how I expected her to reciprocate from behind a countertop-to-ceiling Perspex panel with just a small slot for payment at the bottom.

'Well, hello, Alice Carroll. I'm Suki Price. Best of luck with Nell's shop. Take it from me, it's not easy being a shopkeeper around here.'

'I've bought Nell's cottage,' I began.

She gave a bark of joyless laughter. 'I know, but it'll take years before people stop calling it Nell's shop. We don't go by door numbers like you townies do, not least because our cottages aren't numbered. Only the houses in modern developments like the one that awful Terence Bolt's building next to you have door numbers. The proper old houses round here have names, not numbers, apart from in their postcodes.'

She sank her hands into the deep pocket of her apron, which was branded to match the logo above her shopfront.

'That's one of the few things that's all right about this godawful place. All the old houses are different, from the little cottages like yours and mine, to the Big House that Andrew Fancy Gloster lives in.'

The way she spat out the B and the H, Andrew's home sounded like a capitalised name.

'Or the old place Bob Sponge has done up all poncy,' she added.

When she mentioned my neighbour, I couldn't help but picture the pineapple inhabited by the bright-yellow cartoon character, although of course I'd guessed it must be his nickname. I knew from my work at the museum that pineapples were historically symbols of wealth, brought back by successful merchant traders from the Caribbean. Once on holiday in Scotland, I'd seen an old house topped by a pineapple-shaped dome. Was Bob Sponge's house similar? That would account for his nickname. Perhaps that was why he had such high walls around his property – to avoid tourists gawping at it.

'In the olden days, they didn't build houses in tidy rows out here, all looking the same, not like they did in cities. They just threw them up at random, as and when required. Which is another reason why these new houses next to you are going to stick out like a cow in a henhouse. They'll all be those awful "executive" homes.' She pulled her hands out of her apron pocket just long enough to make air quotes.

'Oh no! Are they going to be hideous? And how many will there be?'

'About ten, I think. Old Nutty Bolt's shoehorning five-bed

homes onto plots the size of a bathmat to sell to rich, daft townies who want low-maintenance courtyards instead of proper country gardens. No disrespect.'

I shuffled my feet. 'I may have just moved from the city centre, but I'm neither rich nor daft. I'm not afraid of a bit of gardening, either.'

Well, two out of three of my claims were true. I had no idea how to tame Nell's abandoned jungle. Perhaps the estate agent had been right on that score: I could just pass it off as rewilded.

'But I'm dismayed to hear they're putting up so many new homes next to mine, or any homes at all. Today's the first I've heard of it.'

'Old Dr Foster been filling you in, has he?' She shot me a pitying glance. 'Andrew Gloster, I mean, old gossip that he is. How he ever kept to the Official Secrets Act is a mystery to me. Or p'raps he didn't. I'm hoping some military police'll turn up in Little Pride one day and carry him off.'

I wasn't sure how to answer that. So far Andrew Gloster had been kind to me. If he had a longstanding feud with Suki Price, I wasn't about to take sides, at least not until I knew whose was the best side to be on. I tried to steer our conversation onto safer ground.

'I'm surprised the builder hasn't put up any signage yet. Usually, firms like that are keen to start selling houses off-plan before they've even broken ground.'

'Well, don't be in no hurry,' said Suki. 'Rumour has it he'll be bringing in his workforce this week. Better make the most of the peace and quiet while you've still got it.'

The bell above the shop door jangled as a few schoolchildren pushed and shoved each other on their way in. The name of the village primary school was embroidered on their bright-red sweaters, above a shield that incorporated what looked like a sledgehammer and a scythe, reminiscent of the old USSR flag.

Keeping a surreptitious eye on them as they clustered around boxes of loose pocket-money sweets, Suki raised her voice to be heard above their babble.

'So did you want to buy something, Alice Carroll, or did you just swing by because you couldn't find your way home?'

Even if I hadn't been planning to make a purchase, I would have to make one now, to keep in her good books. Like Andrew Gloster, Suki was in a powerful position to broadcast her first impressions of me to the rest of the community. Maybe that was how she got away with being so rude: no one wanted to fall out with her. That, plus she ran the only shop in the village, apart from mine.

'Actually, I came in for a copy of the *Little Pride Parish News.*'

She peeled one off the neat pile on top of the counter on her side of the Perspex screen. 'That's a pound, please.'

I scrabbled in my purse for the right change and slid a few coins under the screen. She prised the top off an old margarine tub, stickered with a label neatly hand-lettered *LPPN* in indelible pen, and dropped the coins inside. When she set the tub back on the shelf behind her, I noticed a row of similar collecting pots, all with different labels.

As I turned to leave the shop, a chorus of young voices rose up from the queue of red-sweatered children that had formed behind me.

'Hello, Nell! Hello, Miss Little!'

Each child was clutching a tiny white paper bag filled with carefully chosen penny sweets. Together they gazed at me, clearly expecting a reply.

'Hello, children,' I said in my brightest museum voice. 'Actually my name's Alice Carroll.'

'No, you're not, you're the new Nellie!' cried the tallest boy at the back.

All of them fell about laughing, before breaking into a chorus of 'Nellie the Elephant', which was an old song even when I was their age. I guessed old habits died hard in these parts.

I gave them as pleasant a smile as I could muster. As I left the shop, cries of 'Goodbye, Nellie!' and 'Farewell, Nell!' drifted down the high street behind me.

As I turned the key in my front door, it dawned on me that village children may have been taunting Nell Little in this way for generations. How would I ever have a chance of shaking off her long shadow?

I shoved the door open so hard that the door knocker rattled as if to announce a visitor. That rather spooked me.

'This is *my* home!' I shouted, as I flung the *Little Pride Parish News* on the dining table, although no one was there to hear me, unless Nell's ghost was lurking somewhere about the place. 'And over my dead body, as well as Nell's, will I let anyone turn me out of here!'

I just hoped it wouldn't come to that.

10

THE BIG CHOP

Next morning, as I carried a cup of tea to the kitchen table, I caught sight of my dishevelled state in the octagonal, bevel-edged mirror that hung from a chain above the dining-room fireplace. It was far too long since I'd visited a hairdresser. I was conscious I'd rather let myself go since Steven's announcement, not only because of the emotional trauma but also due to the pressure of time on trying to move house while holding down a full-time job. My hair now reached below my shoulders, where numerous split ends tapered to a series of points. I'd aged ten years since Steven had left. If I didn't tidy myself up, the locals wouldn't be calling me the new Nell – they'd be mistaking for the old one.

As I drank my tea, I was flicking through the *Little Pride Parish News* to gather more clues as to the nature of this community when I spotted an advertisement for Coralie's Curls, the village hairdressing salon.

In my newly unemployed state, I couldn't justify splashing out on an expensive city-centre salon, nor could I currently drive to one I assumed a local place like Coralie's Curls would be more affordable. I'd met so few of my new neighbours so far that I still had time to make a first impression on most of the village. A good haircut could only help.

I might also have been seeking distractions to put off sifting through Nell Little's leavings before I could properly unpack my own stuff. But my mind was made up. I punched the salon's telephone number into my mobile phone and headed out of the back door before pressing the dial button. Mobile signals would not penetrate the thick, stone walls of my old cottage, and the best place to send text messages or make calls was standing in the middle of the vegetable patch.

A sweet, sing-song voice answered. 'Coralie's Curls. Coralie speaking.'

I liked her at once.

'Hello, my name's Alice Carroll, and I've just moved here. I wondered whether you have any appointments available this afternoon, please?'

'Ah, so you're the new Nell!' My heart sank, until her next words redeemed her. 'Hello, Alice, and welcome. I'm just doing a couple of after-school kids' trims, but if you'd like to drop in at about four, I'll make you my last appointment of the day. I'll stay as long as you need, and whatever you want done, I can do it.'

I thought, *I could do with more friends with your attitude*, but I said, 'Fabulous! See you at four.'

Coralie's Curls was tucked away in what looked like a small, repurposed barn in Strumpet's Patch. This narrow lane off the high street was lined with higgledy-piggledy rows of low, unnumbered cottages. They looked like modest two-up, two-down homes built to house farm labourers' families when the surrounding fields were still worked by human hand and horse. Between two terraces of cottages lay a green space given over to an immaculate vegetable plot. At the bottom of a beaten cinder path lay a small stone barn that housed Coralie's Curls. As I strolled down the path, I admired neat rows of bean-pole wigwams hung with slender pods and shoulder-high raspberry canes whose tight nuggets of lime-green fruit were tinged with pale pink.

The low Cotswold stone structure looked the polar opposite of the sleek beauty salons I was used to in town, with their huge, plate-glass windows, rented palm trees and leather sofas. The entrance to Coralie's Curls was a wooden stable door with the top half fastened back. I would not have been surprised to find myself in a sheep-shearing shed, where a sturdy yokel was waiting to greet me bran-dishing wool clippers.

Instead, I discovered a pretty, light, new-age style setting, with sunshine streaming in through Velux roof windows that I hadn't noticed on my approach. Along the far wall stood a row of old-fash-ioned pine carver chairs on swivel bases, their seats softened by floral prints reminiscent of the sixties and seventies. Large mirrors with pine frames hung on the wall above antique, marble-topped washstands. The undulating flagstone floor gleamed in the sunlight, well scrubbed to remove any traces of the barn's previous four-legged residents.

The other walls were brightened by woven hangings and patch-work quilts in a kaleidoscope of colours. They must have warmed the place up in winter, and on this early summer's day, they were a fresh, bright contrast to the muted old stone. It felt like a safe retreat.

Coralie jumped out from a vast wicker egg chair suspended from the ceiling by a thick, dark rope and lined with well-worn sheepskins. The promise of a turn in the swing seat must have encouraged even the most reluctant child to allow Coralie to cut their hair. Even at my age, I had a sudden urge to climb into it myself, not to play, but to turn to face the corner, hiding from the worries that were crowding in on me. I hoped a decent haircut would make me braver and stronger – a kind of reverse Samson effect.

'Hi there, you must be Alice,' said Coralie brightly, gesturing to one of the pine chairs. 'Have a seat and we'll get you gowned up.'

I hesitated before sitting down.

'That's a beautiful cushion,' I remarked. 'It seems a shame to cover it up with my bottom.'

Coralie laughed. 'You'd soon change your mind if I removed it. These chairs are rock-hard without extra padding. But thanks, anyway. I make the cushions myself in idle moments – the wall hangings, quilts and flower arrangements too.'

She gestured towards the low ceiling, where wreaths, bouquets and ropes of colourful dried flowers garlanded the ancient, pitted rafters. Between them, tie-dyed scarves were strung like bunting, their muted shades suggesting natural dyes, perhaps brewed from the contents of her garden.

'If you see anything you fancy to brighten up your new home, just ask the price. But no pressure. Moving house is an expensive business, and I shan't be offended if you don't.'

From a wicker basket in the corner of the barn she produced an old hessian flour sack, its shorter seam unpicked, and ribbons stitched to the corners to create a cape. She draped it around my shoulders and secured it at my throat with a large bow.

Laying her hands gently on the sides of my head, she made me confront my reflection in the mirror. My hair looked as sad as I had been feeling lately. I averted my gaze.

'I just wanted it tidied up, really. Please chop off as much as necessary to get it back into good condition.'

Coralie nodded agreement before seizing a small brass plant spray and squirting the contents all over my hair.

'That'll get rid of any greenfly for starters.' In the mirror, she grinned at my aghast expression. 'Only kidding. It's just nice, soft rainwater to damp it down. The piped water's really hard around here, what with all the limestone in the soil. Water comes out of the tap practically in lumps.' She brandished the plant sprayer again. 'I bought this from your shop, actually. I like upcycling old stuff, finding new uses for vintage things. I was one of Nell Little's best customers. I was so sorry to see her go.'

She picked up a chunky, wide-toothed comb that looked as if she'd carved it herself from an old bone. As I tried not to wonder which animal she'd upcycled it from, she misread my wary look.

'Don't worry, I use a different comb for the nitty kids.'

Just what I needed – another worry for my list.

'Anyway, sad though I am that we've lost dear old Nell Little, I'm very glad you're here now,' she continued cheerfully. 'I'm guessing you'll have a fair bit of dusting to do before you can reopen the shop, but at least you'll have no shortage of stock. I hope the pair of Art Deco green glass vases I had my eye on are still there. Do save them for me if you spot them. They're shaped like bunches of bulrushes – very distinctive.'

Having combed my dampened hair die-straight, she seized a pair of silver scissors with handles fashioned like a stork in flight. That was a relief. I was half expecting her to produce a pair of garden shears to go with my sacking cape.

'These came from Nell's too.'

I decided I'd better come clean about my intentions.

'To be honest, Coralie, I hadn't originally planned to reopen the shop, but it seems I'm going to have to, unless I can get change of use granted by the local council. The man who runs the parish magazine, Andrew Gloster, told me this morning it might be tricky if not impossible, to get planning consent for change of use.'

Coralie nodded. 'Yes, that's why you got the place so cheap. Didn't your solicitor pick that up? That was a bit remiss of him.'

I gave a vague nod. I knew people often confide their problems in their hairdressers, but I wasn't ready to share the whole story with someone I barely knew.

'Still, it needn't be such a big problem,' she continued. 'You don't have to open your shop all day, every day, only whenever you want to, like I do with my salon. I'd go mad if I was cutting hair twenty-four-seven. That's what Nell did too. She just opened up when she was in the mood. That's all you need to keep you on the right side of the council. And, as a bonus, it'll really hack off old Nutty Bolt next door. He was livid when the estate agent sold Nell's place to you instead of him.'

'Even though he couldn't get planning permission to convert it to purely residential use?'

'Nah. He's smug, that one. He thought once he'd bought it, the council would weaken. With a bit of help from, you know...' She held up her scissor-free hand, rubbing her thumb across her finger-tips to indicate money. 'Selfish, capitalist git. I wouldn't trust him further than a horse could throw him. If you ask me, he's far too matey with certain influential councillors, parish and local authority.'

'Andrew told me as much himself, though not in quite those terms.'

She nodded. 'What's more, if you don't watch him, he'll be moving your boundary wall in the dead of night and stealing half your garden. You may laugh, but I heard he tried that in another village near here – Wendlebury Barrow, on the Slate Green road. He almost got away with it, too.'

After snipping an inch off the length of my hair, Coralie held up he newly chopped ends of a clump to the light and wrinkled her nose in dissatisfaction. She started to go round again, taking off a further inch.

'There's no love lost between me and old Nutcase,' she continued. 'Not since he tried to turf me off my land here for another of his blooming development projects, but I sent him packing. The ancient deeds of this plot ensure it can only be used for agriculture and associated services. Hence my kitchen garden and the flowers above your head and all the sheepy stuff. Technically, the hairdressing is a chargeable hobby, but between you and me, it makes me more money than selling the stuff I grow and the crafts I make. Then when I thwarted him, Bolt turned nasty. Tried to have my salon shut down on health and safety grounds. When that failed, he started some hideous rumour that I wasn't safe around children.' She waved her open scissors in the air in anger. 'Besides, I work my curls off in my smallholding. I've earned the right to stay here.'

'You don't live on the premises, then?' I queried, looking up to the loft space. I pictured her camping out on the mezzanine, sleeping on bales of hay.

When she clamped her strong hands on either side of my head and pointed my face back at the mirror, I didn't resist. Her scissors looked very sharp, and I didn't want to cause any slips.

'Oh no,' she replied. 'I live in a tiny house.'

'Which one? They all look pretty tiny down this lane.'

'Not a tiny *house*. A *tiny* house. You must have seen them on Instagram – people turning really small spaces into compact homes. Mine's an old shepherd's hut on wheels, tucked out of sight behind the salon. But I call it a tiny house, so it doesn't sound as posh as the shepherd's hut David Cameron famously wrote his memoirs in.'

I laughed. I couldn't imagine she and the former prime minister had anything else in common.

'Come and have a coffee in my tiny house sometime, and I'll show you the rest of my haul from Nell's shop.'

'Thanks, I'd like that.'

The more of my hair she sheared, the more I warmed to her. It was good to have found someone on my own wavelength in the village. Admiring her style, I wondered whether I should try to make my cottage similarly bohemian.

Finally, she seized a hefty silver-backed hand mirror from the washstand in front of us and held it to the back of my head, tilting it to give me a rear view of my new hairstyle in the wall-mounted looking-glass.

I'd been so engrossed in our conversation that I hadn't realised how much she'd chopped off. I was very much the freshly shorn sheep, my hair now clear of my shoulders and level with my chin.

'Lovely,' she declared. 'A whole new you.'

'One I didn't even know was lurking underneath all that hair,' I observed, as she whisked the sacking away from my shoulders and went to shake it onto the garden through the top half of the stable door.

'All useful material for nesting birds,' she remarked. 'And what the birds don't take makes good fertiliser for my fruit and veg.'

I'd try not to think of that when eating any produce I bought from her. It sounded a little too close to cannibalism for my liking. Suddenly the prospect of those ripening raspberries didn't seem so appetising.

Getting up from the chair, I pulled my purse out of my handbag.

'Cash or card?' I asked, wondering whether she had an electricity supply to power a card machine. In this shrine to all things vintage, I had half-expected her to offer me a blow-dry with a pair of blacksmith's bellows.

'Neither,' she replied. 'You can pay me in kind with those green glass vases when you find them. That's how Nell always paid for her hairdos.'

For the amount of stuff in Coralie's salon that had come from Nell's, never mind the contents of her tiny house, Nell Little must either have been exceptionally well coiffed or bald.

'Take care, Alice, and watch your back with that toad Terence Bolt,' was Coralie's final piece of advice as I let myself out of the stable door. 'Don't think he'll have given up on you just because you beat him in the race to buy the Cotswold Curiosity Shop. He'll be out to oust you one way or another. Stand firm.'

I was left feeling liberated my sleek bob symbolic of freedom and fresh beginnings. As I headed for my cottage, I ran my hand over my bare neck, trying to dismiss the prickling sensation that had just run down my spine. It must just be that some stray snippets of loose hair have fallen inside my top, I told myself. But as I approached my cottage, something about it looked different, and it took me a moment to work out what it was.

In my absence, the *Sold* sign had disappeared from my front garden – which was good, because its absence symbolised that I was here to stay – and along the front wall of the paddock, a new, much larger wooden board had been installed, announcing the immediate commencement of work on Paddock Close:

An exciting new development of ten executive homes for the discerning buyer.

11

MISTAKEN IDENTITY

As I put my key in the lock, I heard a tremulous voice calling, 'Good afternoon' to me from the direction of the pavement.

'Hello, and welcome to Little Pride.'

The old lady who had accosted me about my car parking ability yesterday was hobbling up the path in her outsized boots. For a moment, I wondered whether she was about to present me with a poisoned apple, like Snow White's wicked stepmother.

As she approached, she waved her walking stick at me, but thankfully this time it seemed to be in greeting rather than in anger.

'I'm very glad to see you're here to take charge at last. Have you managed to chase out those unsavoury squatters I saw here yesterday?'

Squatters? I knew the house was cluttered, but surely I'd have spotted any surplus human beings in the cottage.

She seemed to recognise my confusion.

'Ah, they must have fled the scene before you arrived. I see their beaten-up old car's gone too. Good riddance, say I, to an awful, lovely pair. He was half-naked at midday, and possibly half-cut too, by the look of him. On drugs, too, I expect. That potty stuff, no doubt. He looked African but I don't know where she was from. Somewhere from that Europe, no doubt. Not from round here, that's for sure.'

With a start, I realised she was talking about Danny and me.

'Parked their car all over the place, too. No regard for the people what lives here. It's bad enough having that blessed Bolt desiccating the old paddock next door.' She raised her voice, presumably hoping he'd hear. 'He didn't oughta go building houses to get more townie types into Little Pride. We got more than enough of them already. Still, I hope you're settling in, dearie?'

'Yes, thank you.' I spoke a little stiffly, wary of giving the game away. Hoping she wouldn't recognise my voice from our earlier conversation, I tried to speak lower than usual to disguise it.

'You got your work cut out for you, getting Nell Little's shop up together for reopening.'

'Actually, it's—' But she didn't let me finish.

'Don't you worry, we'll still support you once it's up and running. A nice little earner, Nell's shop is. And you're young enough to have the energy to make even more of it than she did. Best of luck to you, my dear.'

'Thank you.' Calling me young wrongfooted me. I suppose I was, compared to her. Perhaps she and Nell had been contemporaries. My visitor was at least eighty. I told her what I thought she'd want to hear. 'I'll look forward to seeing you in my shop, then.'

Her copious wrinkles deepened as she gave me a gratified grin baring a few witchy, yellow teeth. Then she pivoted about her walking stick and stomped back down the path.

As I stepped over the threshold, I spotted an old-fashioned correspondence card on the doormat. The address was a single line in printed cursive:

The Big House, Little Pride, Gloucestershire.

There was no postcode, as if The Big House were so well known that the postman could find it without. Even Buckingham Palace and Windsor Castle have postcodes.

When I began to read the handwritten message, I nearly dropped the card in fright.

You've got until midday tomorrow

What sort of threat was this?

I shook my head at my own feebleness. The events of the last few days had made me jumpy. I'd need to pull myself together if I was going to make a fresh start. Failure was not an option. I braced myself to read on.

to submit your entry for this month's Little Pride Parish News. *It goes off to the printers on Monday, so if you'd kindly tell me your new opening times, I can squeeze them into this issue. Also, the offer of a free ad still stands. £5 per year thereafter.*
Yours, Andrew Gloster

I laughed aloud, partly from relief at my stupid initial assumption that someone was threatening me, and partly at the ridiculously low advertising rate. It made me feel as if I were just playing shops, like Marie Antoinette playing milkmaids, although I didn't have the back-up of Versailles for when I'd had enough.

It was starting to seem inevitable that I'd have to open the shop for a little while each week, at least until I'd managed to persuade the district council to grant change of use. Surely I could make them realise that a chaotic little shop full of old junk off the beaten track couldn't possibly be commercially viable long term, especially if, like Coralie, the locals were used to paying for goods in kind. There were only so many haircuts I could have – and I couldn't pay the bills with hair trimmings.

My visitor had just informed me the shop was a nice little earner, but how on earth had Nell Little survived on its proceeds? Perhaps she had supplemented the shop's takings with her old-age pension. Or perhaps she didn't. Perhaps she died penniless of starvation, albeit with immaculate hair.

I hoped I wouldn't find her ghost haunting my larder in the dead of night, in search of nourishment. That thought would be enough to stop me making midnight raids on the biscuit tin if I woke up feeling peckish. One day, I might be brave enough to ask someone to tell me the circumstances of her demise.

Still, opening the shop temporarily would give me the opportunity to make a little bit of money while I applied for proper jobs. It would also help dispose of the goods she'd left without having to heft it all to the tip or to charity shops – not easy in the absence of my car or, heaven forbid, my driving licence.

I'd have to take cash, as there was no sign of an electronic payment system anywhere in the shop. On the shop counter stood a huge, old, brass, mechanical cash register. I half-expected it to work in old money – the pounds, shillings and pence from before decimalisation.

I could treat my temporary opening as a giant yard sale, but in more comfortable, weatherproof surroundings. If I couldn't shift it all, as a last resort, I could bring in a house-clearance service. One way or another, I was determined to achieve my dream of a neat, tidy, minimalist home.

I wandered through to the dining room to set Andrew's note on the little roll-top desk that Nell had left behind. Then I returned to the shop to consider my priorities.

Underneath all the dust, there were signs that this had once been a very attractive, quaint and interesting treasure trove. The room was full of character and filled with gentle, natural light from the bay window. If I worked at it, I could make it quite pleasant. Nell was going up in my estimation.

I decided to set an opening date, as Andrew Gloster had suggested, choosing a day that would allow me plenty of time to get organised. Committing to opening the shop and advertising regular hours would give me the impetus I needed to get stuck into sorting it all out – something I'd have to do sooner or later if I wasn't to end up skulking permanently among the cobwebs like a latter-day Miss Havisham.

Thus resolved, I returned to the dining room and opened up the roll-top bureau. It seemed Nell used it to write up the shop's accounts. Tucked into the upright cubbyholes were half-used receipt books and old-fashioned double-entry bookkeeping ledgers. On the left was a bundle of slightly foxed, deckle-edged correspondence cards in a delicate, duck-egg blue. I extracted one to examine it. If they didn't bear her name, but just the address, I might be able to use them myself. At the top were two rows in Courier font reminiscent of vintage typewriter script. The top row, in upper case, read:

THE COTSWOLD CURIOSITY SHOP

The address below was minus its postcode, and its telephone number consisted of just three figures: 262. It must have been printed back when far fewer people had landlines and numbers were much shorter – just the local exchange followed by three numbers. Perhaps in those days, phone calls still had to be placed through an operator.

Even so, the cards would be useful for any notes I needed to send in the village, where everybody would know where the shop was without its postcode to put into their satnavs. They'd also know to add the modern prefix to the old three-figure number. The numbers for Coralie's Curls, Suki's Stores and Andrew all started with the same first three numbers as mine – the village's area code.

I picked up Nell's old, red, lacquered fountain pen from the pretty brass tray on top of the bureau, but of course it was too dried-up to use. I wondered what the last thing was that she had written with it. Her will, perhaps?

I set the pen back on the tray, planning to try to restore it later. It was a decent pen, very saleable in working order. Instead, I grabbed a plastic museum ballpoint from my handbag and sat down to compose a reply to Andrew. I couldn't wait to see what my opening day might bring.

12

PLANNING AHEAD

A few days after the new July issue of the *Little Pride Parish News* had been delivered, I buttonholed Andrew Gloster in Suki's Stores.

'Andrew, was it you who told the district council I'm about to reopen my shop?'

Tucking a copy of the *Daily Telegraph* under his arm, Andrew gazed at me in surprise.

'My dear, I don't know what you mean. It's not my place to invite them to anything. But of course, the district council's communications officer reads each issue of the *Little Pride Parish News*. It's the perfect way for him to keep an eye on goings-on here, and then he disseminates its news to the appropriate members of the council.'

Suki coughed to remind him to hand over the payment for his newspaper. When he dropped a handful of coins onto the counter without looking at her, she refused to let him exclude her from the conversation.

'Yes, and that's how they cottoned on to poor old Reg Pettifer's illegal conversion of his pigsty. They saw he'd started advertising it in the mag as a holiday let for villagers' friends and relations. The people in planning made him strip it all out again and restore it to its original agricultural use. Nearly broke the bank for him, all that investment wasted, and him just trying to diversify to supplement his family income. I bet that made you happy, Andy? All that power invested in your poxy paper?'

'My name is Andrew, as you well know,' he retorted, still keeping his back to her.

'Not to mention what it did to poor old Reg up here.' Suki rolled her eyes as she tapped her temple with her forefinger. 'Went clean round the bend for a while, camping out in the pigsty hisself for a bit, like the hog that he is.'

I wondered whether Andrew felt responsible for Reg's plight, or even guilty.

'It's all very well assuming that because we're in the middle of nowhere, and our streets aren't riddled with surveillance cameras, that we can do whatever we like,' he retorted. 'The rules are clear. The good people at the council are only doing their jobs.'

Suki was unabashed. 'Not that they'll do anything about anything if they don't want to. You only have to count the potholes in the lanes to know that. But if there's something in it for them, they're all over it like measles.'

Andrew ignored her. 'So, am I to gather the planning officers have been in touch with you, Alice?'

I produced a sheet of council letterhead from my handbag and shook the folds out. 'Yes. I've just received an unsolicited letter apologising that they're unable to attend my reopening, even though I didn't invite them. I wouldn't even know who from the council to invite if I wanted to. Do you think they're trying to catch me out?'

When I held out the letter for him to read, his lips twitched in amusement. 'I very much doubt it. We all want to see the Cotswold Curiosity Shop succeed under its new management, don't we Suki?'

Now that he was actively involving her, she chose to ignore him.

'I believe they have just taken a rather formal approach to the open invitation you put in your advert in the *Parish News*,' Andrew continued.

'Ain't got nothing better to do than write pointless letters, the idle so-and-sos,' grumbled Suki. 'Good excuse for not doing what they should be doing, like fixing potholes. I bet they won't come out on a Saturday, neither, outside their office hours.'

'So, my advice to you, Alice,' Andrew continued smoothly, as if Suki hadn't spoken, 'is to make sure when you reopen your shop, it's squeaky clean and safe, because if they spot a trip hazard or a contravention of fire regulations, they'll be down on you like a ton of Cotswold stone.'

'But surely they will be on my side as their stated policy is to keep local shops open?' I replied.

Suki tossed her head. 'And I'm Britney Spears. If I were you, Alice Carroll, like Andy here says, I'd suck up to those councillors for all you're worth. You can be as rude as you like about them after they've gone.'

Andrew finally deigned to reply to her. 'That isn't quite what I said, Suki. But the essence is the same. You need to avoid upsetting the council, whether you're bent on making your shop a success or whether you want to apply for change of use and return it to residential use. The choice is yours.'

13

BLOWING AWAY THE COBWEBS

To my housework-averse mother's perpetual surprise, I've always been very good at cleaning and tidying, and this was one reason I'd been looking forward to making my new home minimalist. It would be so much easier to keep it straight and spotless without Steven's clutter. An obsessive completist, he was constantly acquiring new supposed treasures for his collection of the moment, but somehow never found the time to dust or polish his displays. This was particularly annoying when so many of them involved intricate carvings such as chess sets or netsuke, those tiny Japanese sculptures used as toggles. At least most of the things he collected were on a small scale – no suits of armour or weaponry. He had the grace to be grateful for my expert ministrations, using the specialist skills I'd learned in my work at the museum, but they also gave him a handy excuse to leave all the cleaning to me.

The first time Mum saw Steven's bachelor flat, she murmured so only I could hear, 'Are you sure, dear?'

Still thinking he was my soulmate, I replied cheerily, 'Consider it the attraction of opposites, Mum.' I was just glad to have found a boyfriend who was more interested in history than football.

With a pang of guilt, I realised now that I'd barely spoken to Mum in the last few months, perhaps feeling guilty for letting her down with my break-up – or for proving she'd been right about Steven all along. No parent wants to see their child heartbroken. In truth, I'd been spending less time with her for the last decade, since I'd finally accepted I'd never be able to give her the grandchildren she longed for. I decided to make amends by inviting her to stay as soon as I'd fixed up the spare bedroom.

But first, I had the shop to revamp.

Although not exactly relishing making the Cotswold Curiosity Shop fit for the public – and the prying eyes of the council officers – I knew I could do it. Quite apart from my experience at the museum, on moving into Steven's bachelor flat, I'd made it hygienic, safe and habitable while preserving the integrity of his collections. When we upsized to our three-bedroomed house, I'd assumed the extra space would absorb his clutter while leaving plenty of clear living space for me. I even suggested he use the larger spare bedroom to house it all, naively assuming that would stop it spilling over into the rest of the house.

He reciprocated by offering me the boxroom for my needle-crafts – I'm passionate about knitting and crochet – and I never set so much as a ball of wool outside my precious space. His collections, on the other hand, free-ranged about the house like chickens in an orchard, and they were as impossible to round up without more escaping. Secretly, I often yearned to play the fox.

So, with the shop's reopening date less than three weeks away, I got stuck into the task of first giving the shop a thorough clean, then rearranging the goods for sale. Many items were inexplicably dishevelled – a handsome pair of brass candlesticks had fallen over and been left on their sides, a tin of antique buttons had scattered its contents on the floor, and an enamel dish that must have once held old brooches now stood empty in the middle of a pool of them, as if a tiny puppy had leaped into the dish and dug them all out with scurrying paws.

Presuming Nell Little had everything in good order up until her last day of trading, how had it got in such a state? Had she lost competence as she aged, or even, perish the thought, had some kind of death throes in the shop that made her flail about, sending everything flying? Why had nobody tidied it up? Surely she would have left the shop to somebody. That somebody should have had the sense to restore order to make the property more saleable.

Even once everything was the right way up and so clean it was gleaming in the sunshine filtering in through the bottle-glass windows, the display didn't show off the goods to best advantage. Nell seemed to have put everything wherever there was a space, rather than sorting goods by function or colour. The result was a higgledy-piggledy mosaic in which nothing really stood out.

Rainbow order, I decided. That would add pizzazz. Plus, rainbows were an emblem of hope, promise and good luck. I was going to need all of those things if I was going to make a go of the shop until I found a new job.

And I really ought to start looking for a job before too long, before I get too used to a life of leisure, I scolded myself, arranging bone-china plates in colour order on a wall-mounted pine rack. *I just need to get my ducks – and glassware and hats and beads and brooches – in a neat row first.*

As I slowly breathed new life into Nell Little's stock, my opinion of it morphed from disdain into admiration. I could see the beauty in inter-war pressed glass vases and dressing-table sets once they were clean enough to catch the light.

I located the pair of green glass vases Coralie had asked for, and I set them on the counter by the till and labelled them *sold*, adding her name. My first sale – in kind, anyway. How to celebrate?

On a whim, I filled them with branches of white lilac from the back garden. Then I wrote a note on one of Nell's correspondence cards, inviting her to come and collect them. After I'd had enough of cleaning for one day, I strolled round to Coralie's Curls, which had already closed for the day. Too shy to delve behind the barn to seek out her tiny house, I slipped the card between the top and bottom panels of the salon's stable door. If I could lure the artistic Coralie into the shop and gain her approval of the changes I was making, I'd be more confident that other locals would love it too.

Hang on, I thought. *You've changed your tune. Why does anyone's opinion matter when what you really want is to close the shop for good? Wouldn't it be more helpful to your change-of-use application if all the villagers stayed away? That would prove the shop wasn't commercially viable.*

But somehow, now that I'd purged the shop of so much dust and grime, and everything was basking in sunshine, the spirit of Nell Little was starting to get under my skin.

14

BARNABY'S BOTTLES

A couple of days before my official opening, I was bustling about the shop with a duster, with the door propped open for fresh air, when a tall, broad chap with a blonde buzz cut and a surprisingly tanned complexion for an English summer strolled into the shop carrying a large, orange plastic bucket full of muddy glass bottles, some clear, others in jewel-like blues and greens.

With a cheery 'Hello, love,' he swung the bucket onto the counter, nearly sending my laptop flying. 'Present for you, love. Just dug this little lot up breaking the ground next door for the first house. The boss told me to stop fussing and chuck 'em in the skip but I thought they might be worth something to you, as they look a bit old. So, I sneaked a spadeful into this bucket when he wasn't looking, and here they are.'

He lifted an old-fashioned clear glass lemonade bottle out of the bucket to show me. It was the type sealed with a marble that fell inside when the drink was gone. He gave it a vigorous shake rattling the marble against the thick glass for effect.

I pointed to the lower shelf of a big pine dresser to his left where I'd lined up half a dozen of the same kind of bottle.

'Well, there you go. You can sell 'em in sets.'

He grinned, revealing teeth like patio paving slabs. Everything about him seemed as sturdy as a bulldozer. Bolt was lucky to have him.

'How much did you want for them?' I asked, glad of the chance to get him on my side. A spy in Bolt's camp would be useful. I opened the cash drawer of the till. 'In this case, I'd be happy to pay cash.'

He dropped the bottle back into the bucket with a clatter. 'Oh, I don't want no money for 'em. They're old rubbish as far as I'm concerned, but all the same, I'm glad to find them a new home. Better'n dumping 'em. Old Nuts and Bolts might not give a toss about the environment, but I don't like to chuck out stuff that's still got life left in it.'

When he rested his elbows on the counter and leaned towards me, I sensed a 'but' coming.

'But if you were to offer me a coffee and a piece of cake by way of a thank you, I wouldn't object. Forgot me lunch today, and it's me tea break now. Thought it would be nice to spend it in here. Gets me out of the way of the boss for a bit.'

Whatever I sold those bottles for – and I thought they'd probably prove popular with tourists once I'd cleaned them up – the dozen or so he'd brought me would have to be worth more than a cup of a tea and a slice of cake. This felt like a win. While he browsed the shop with the air of a bemused museum visitor rather than someone looking to buy, I went to make him a pot of tea and cut a generous slice of Victoria sponge. I didn't ask whether he wanted 'builder's tea', as people often do. As an actual builder, he presumably liked it strong, with plenty of sugar for energy.

When I returned, he was holding in his great hand a coaster made from shards of willow-patterned china. The fragments were arranged in an attractive mosaic, the pieces with the darkest blue in the centre, and the predominantly white around the outside. It was one of several coasters Coralie had made from broken crockery she'd found while digging on her allotment. I told her I thought they'd sell well in my shop, and she was glad of the opportunity.

'We're digging up loads of this sort of stuff too,' he said, replacing the coaster where he'd found it. 'I can bring you more broken crocks, if you like. Round here, before the council invented dustmen, people used to bury all their old household rubbish in their gardens. We find loads of bits like this when we're breaking ground on new sites round this way.'

'So my friend Coralie was telling me.'

It felt good to be able to refer to a local as a friend.

'Shall I bring some round in my lunch break? Swap 'em for a sandwich?'

That seemed a good deal. After all, I wasn't going to sell him a sandwich. This was just a bit of good old-fashioned bartering. Besides, it might please Coralie if I gave her his findings, so she could make some more coasters for me.

Once Barnaby had finished his tea break – we were on first-name terms by the time he left – I lugged the bucket of bottles into the back garden and filled an old tin bath I'd found in the vegetable plot with water from the nearest rain barrel. I submerged the bottles one by one, examining each as I did so. Although the few on the top were old clear lemonade bottles like the sample he'd shown me, further down the bucket were opaque, hexagonal blue and green ones with five ribbed sides and one smooth one embossed with the word *POISON*. From my work at the museum, I judged them to be mid-Victorian, or Edwardian at the latest. I left them there to soak the worst of the dirt off.

As I returned to the shop, I heard footsteps on the hardstanding in front of the shop. Andrew Gloster was approaching the shop door.

'Hi, Andrew, I'm so glad to see you,' I said brightly, closing the lid of my laptop. 'I wanted to thank you for tipping me off about the power of the parish magazine. I haven't had time to do any other advertising, so without your help, I'd have been stuck.'

Really, there was so much to do besides actually manning the shop that I was going to struggle to find time to start applying for proper jobs.

Andrew chuckled. 'You haven't reckoned on the village grapevine and the general nosiness of your new neighbours. They're all gagging for the chance to get inside the shop to see what you've done to the place.'

'Really? I'd have thought it was obvious from looking through the shop window.'

'Yes, but they want to look at the prices, to see whether you've hoiked them all up since Nell's day. Plus, they want to meet you for themselves, especially after a rumour got about that blonde triplets and a black man had moved into your cottage.'

'Triplets? Where on earth did that idea come from?'

'Apparently, people have described three very similar blonde women associated with the house, each with a different hairstyle. Speculation's rife as to the sleeping arrangements for the four of you in a two-bedroomed cottage.'

I couldn't help but laugh at the ridiculous notion.

'It's correct about the black man, at least. He's my friend Danny, who I used to work with at the city museum, but he doesn't live with me. He's just been very kindly helping me out. He was here on Saturday afternoon for a bit too. But where are my two supposed sisters? Shirking again?'

I made a show of looking around, as if they might suddenly spring out from behind the decoupage screen.

He smirked. 'The first one was a bit slovenly, apparently, with long, tangly hair, and still in her pyjamas at noon.'

Embarrassed, I covered my face with my hands. 'That'd be me. A couple of days after I'd moved in, I'd been having a lie-in when Maudie Frampton knocked at my door to complain about my parking. Danny happened to be sleeping over – on the couch – as he'd driven me home from my leaving do the night before.'

Strictly speaking, it wasn't my leaving do, but it sounded better that way.

'Then there was a tidier, long-haired version, all freshly scrubbed and chatting to me at the bus stop.'

I nodded. That made sense.

'But the woman since seen cleaning up the shop since the squatter sisters left had a much shorter haircut, although very similar otherwise.'

'Thanks to Coralie's Curls,' I replied, tossing my neat bob.

'So, my reason for visiting now,' he began, with a twinkle in his eye, 'is to ask whether the three of you might like to collaborate on a monthly column for the parish magazine? Maybe highlighting a different object in the shop each time? It might even help you sell it.'

'I'll confer with my sisters and let you know,' I said gravely. 'But I'm sure one of us would love to. And whichever one does, I can help them put it in historical context. From the many years I worked at Broadwick City Museum, I have a special interest in Victorian domestic social history, which, now I think about it, is the perfect background for running a shop like this.'

'It's almost as if it was meant to be,' he replied solemnly.

Was Andrew flirting with me now too? I'd have to ask Coralie about his marital status. Not that I was necessarily interested in him in that way, but if he was married, I didn't want to encourage him. I supposed he might be single, assuming working spies don't have much opportunity for romance and marriage. Living now in a remote village like this might not give him the chance to meet many eligible women, if indeed he was interested in women.

For a moment, I felt sorry for him. Then I realised I'd be in a similar position. There were no single people's apartments in Little Pride, like there were in the city. All the homes were family-sized, like the proposed new-builds next door. How much better it would be if Bolt were building one-bedroom apartments.

I was just wondering where this conversation would go next when Barnaby came marching up the path. The cardboard box he was carrying rattled as he approached the counter. Again, he slammed it down. I was getting the impression he couldn't do anything gently. I decided I'd better give him a chunky stoneware mug for his lunchtime brew – one of the Cornishware set on the sideboard – rather than the dainty floral bone china cups and saucers on the Welsh dresser. In any case, his thick fingers wouldn't fit through a teacup's handle.

'Here you go, love. My latest finds for you. Had to slip in here while the boss wasn't looking, as when I asked him nicely if I could bring you my findings, he said no and told me again to just to chuck 'em on the skip. But I'm not doing that when I can bring a smile to your pretty face by bringing them round here.'

He winked, and I blushed. I was probably old enough to be his mum. Was it something in the local water that was making all the men so nice to me, or some curious new allure instilled by Coralie's haircut?

Andrew, perhaps feeling upstaged, peered into Barnaby's cardboard box.

'Bits of old china, mate,' said Barnaby affably. 'Her friend likes sticking them on placemats, apparently.'

'He means Coralie,' I told Andrew. 'I'm going to stock her mosaic coasters.'

Barnaby turned to me. 'I'll have ham, if you've got it, love. And coffee this time, nice and strong, please.'

Andrew dipped his hand into the cardboard box at random, as if drawing the winning raffle tickets from a hat. He pulled out a palmful of small, straight-edged pieces in shades of terracotta, cream and a soft dark blue.

'Bit small, aren't they? It'll take Coralie ages to make a mosaic out of these. A bit boring too, as they've no pattern, just plain colours.' He gave me a guarded look, as if testing me, though I wasn't sure how.

I waved my hand airily. 'I reckon Coralie could make anything look pretty, given the chance. And if she's not interested, maybe I'll bag them up and sell them as mosaic kits for people to make at home. I'd just pop in a plain square floor tile as a base and some tile cement. We used to sell kits like that in the museum shop when we were hosting a travelling exhibition on Greek and Roman art. Anyone who's a bit crafty like Coralie would snap them up.'

'She's crafty all right,' said Andrew, in a tone that didn't sound exactly complimentary. 'Anyway, must press on, Alice. *Ciao* for now.'

Carelessly, he dropped the pieces of pottery back into the box, except for a couple of pieces that fell on the floor. He stooped to pick them up just as I was asking Barnaby whether he wanted milk and sugar in his coffee. I'm sure he thought I didn't notice that instead of returning them to the box, he slipped them into his jacket pocket.

My first shoplifter! And before I'd even opened for business too. I was so dumbstruck that I didn't think to tackle him. Still, it was only a few pieces of broken pottery, and hardly valuable.

I shrugged it off and went to make Barnaby's lunch, leaving him wandering about the shop with the perplexed air of a child on its first trip to the zoo. At least I could trust Barnaby not to pocket any of my stock.

15

THE GRAND REOPENING

I'd chosen a Saturday to declare the Cotswold Curiosity Shop open again, because I thought the villagers would be more likely to attend than on a weekday, when they might be at work or at school. The retired could of course come any time. I was already pondering ways of encouraging them to visit during the working week. I'd need to work hard to keep my little business afloat between weekends, which I expected to be busier than weekdays. I could use the rest of the time for other purposes, such as a part-time job in the town, Or if the shop proved to be successful, I might even need some weekdays for sourcing stock. Only now was it dawning on me that the shop might provide a full-time job in itself.

On the other hand, my weekends might turn out to be so busy that I might be able to afford to open only on weekends.

Once I'd cleared Nell's inventory, I thought topping up stock would be a challenge. I wondered whether Steven might give me permission to sell the stuff he'd left in storage to reduce or eliminate his warehousing bill. If he was serious about travelling for the rest of his life, the storage costs would be nothing but a drain on his disposable income. What pleasure it would give me to actively dispose of the hated stuff, and at a profit too! Now that I didn't have to see it every day, I realised some of it was actually quite decent, such as his collection of fancy chess sets.

Alternatively, I might start selling my own handicrafts, as Coralie did, without creating direct competition, as my specialities were knitting and crochet and hers were textiles and ceramics. I could also offer to sell some of her work on commission. My shop on the high street would get far more passing trade than her salon tucked away on Strumpet's Patch. Plus, I had space on my side: she couldn't stockpile much in her tiny house, and her hairdressing barn was already full to bursting.

But I was getting ahead of myself. I had yet to welcome my first paying customer.

Half an hour before my chosen opening time, I lit a few strategically placed scented candles to mask any remaining mustiness, then went to the kitchen to fortify myself with one last coffee. When I returned to the shop at ten to ten, I was astonished to see outside the shop door a growing queue of locals, all clutching bulging shopping bags. Surely they hadn't already done a big shop at Suki's Stores, the only retail outlet in the village apart from Coralie's. Perhaps they'd been to a jumble sale at the village hall that no one had told me about. If so, I'd have words with Andrew Gloster for not forewarning me of the clash of dates. But that couldn't be the case. I'd have seen an advertisement for it in the *Parish News*.

I took a deep breath to calm my nerves. Suddenly, I didn't feel ready for this onslaught. There were barely any familiar faces in the queue, apart from Andrew's about halfway down, and Maudie Frampton.

Then Nell's grandfather clock creaked, its squeaky mechanism giving advance warning that it was about to strike the hour. At the first chime, a raucous cry sounded at the shop door. The impatien customers at the front of the queue were shoving each other to open the door before I'd had a chance to unlock it.

They're not being aggressive, I tried to reassure myself. *Just enthusiastic.* Besides, I'd invited the village to come along at ten, and here they were, out in force. I could hardly complain when they were being so supportive.

With another deep breath, I lifted the flap in the counter that separated me from the shop floor and went to unlock the door. Before I'd removed the key from the lock, I was almost flattened by a stampede of eager villagers. After peeling myself off the back of the door, I squeezed past them before barricading myself behind the counter.

Gripping the till with both hands to steady myself, I smiled sweetly at no one in particular and prepared to handle my first transaction. A posh-looking lady in her fifties (so, in her prime, like me), was brandishing a crystal rose bowl topped with silver mesh to aid flower-arranging. I frowned. I didn't recognise it from Nell's stock, nor did it bear one of the cute handwritten manila price tags I'd spent ages affixing to every item.

'So, what will you give me for this precious family heirloom?' she asked briskly.

She set it down so hard on the counter that I feared she'd shatter the crystal.

'I beg your pardon?' I faltered. Had I misheard?

She began to speak more slowly, as if patronising someone with a shaky grasp of the English language. 'How much will you pay me for this valuable collectible?'

Playing for thinking time, I picked it up carefully, turning it around in my hands and holding it up to the morning sunshine. Then the penny dropped, but fortunately not the vase.

'I'm sorry, I think you've come to the wrong place. This isn't some kind of *Antiques Roadshow*. I don't give valuations.'

In disdainful tones that would have done Lady Bracknell proud, she roared, 'Antiques Roadshow? ANTIQUES ROADSHOW?'

A Mexican wave of murmurs spread from the counter to the back of the queue as the other customers tuned in to our conversation. I was relieved to notice that last in line, halfway down the front path, stood Danny.

'My dear,' began Little Pride's answer to Oscar Wilde's creation. 'My dear, did you not know that Nell Little exercised a time-honoured tradition of replenishing her stock by investing in the unwanted accoutrements of her neighbours? She allowed us to liquidate our assets in a mutually beneficial manner. Surely you plan to employ the same *modus operandi*?'

That explained all the bulging carrier bags. This wasn't a queue of eager customers. All these villagers were expecting to sell me their unwanted bric-a-brac.

'Just offer her a tenner to speed things up for the rest of us, darlin',' came a man's voice from amid the crowd, but I refused to be rushed. I didn't want my first transaction to get my new enterprise off on the wrong foot. If I did what she asked, wouldn't everyone else expect the same treatment? I'd taken the precaution of filling the till with a float of a hundred pounds in change, but that wouldn't go very far if everyone in the shop was expecting a hand-out.

'Hang on,' I began slowly, choosing my words with care. I would not allow this rude woman to take advantage of me. 'If this is a family heirloom, it must be worth more than I can offer you.'

Her affronted expression confirmed that I'd called her bluff.

The rotund, rosy-cheeked couple who were next in line fell about laughing as the posh woman grabbed her rose bowl, stuffed it in her wicker basket, and stormed out of the shop, pushing aside those who were blocking the doorway.

I may have just made an enemy, I thought, *but perhaps I've acquired two friends in the process.*

A few feet away, Andrew was grinning as he scribbled notes in a small leather-bound notebook. I hoped this contretemps wasn't about to become the front-page story in the next issue of the *Little Pride Parish News*.

The rosy-cheeked couple edged forward, chuckling.

'That'll teach Madge Lawrence to swallow a dictionary with her breakfast,' declared the man. 'All long words and no manners.'

'And no better than she should be, too, since she married that fancy widower in one o' they new executive homes,' added his wife, clutching her ample stomach in her mirth. 'Why, when she first came to the village, she was living in a caravan and selling pegs door-to-door.'

She shot her husband a mischievous look that made me suspect she was exaggerating.

When he had extracted from his wife's large straw basket a bunch of dried flowers and grasses and laid it gently on the counter, I stopped myself just in time from expressing my thanks for their kind opening-day gift.

'A pound a bunch, Nell Little used to pay us for these,' he explained. 'Then she'd sell 'em on at three quid a time. Went like 'ot cakes, they did. Except they're not edible, of course. You don't want to let no one eat 'em.'

He winked at his wife, and right on cue she let out a throaty chortle. It must have been a laugh a minute in their house.

The dried flowers, all soft roses and golds and mauves and greens, went perfectly with the boho/cottagecore vibe I was aiming for. The several empty vases on display would look much more alluring filled with flowers like these. And if they didn't sell, at least they'd enhance the display.

'I'll take five bunches for starters,' I offered.

'Done!' cried the man.

When he spat on his palm and held it out for me to shake, I froze. I didn't want to appear rude, but...

His wife slapped his arm, but not so hard that he'd have felt it beneath the two thick sweaters he was wearing.

'Don't frighten the poor girl,' she scolded, before turning to me. 'What old Nell used to do now, dearie, is write it down on one of they carbonated tickets in the till.' She nodded towards the great cash register. 'Then she'd give us the top copy and keep the other to make her books balance at the end of the day. It may be olde-worlde' – she pronounced both the final Es – 'but it worked a treat for Nell Little. Mr and Mrs Jorkins, we are.'

When I depressed the *No Sale* key on the till, the cash drawer sprang open, and I peered inside. I'd wondered what that little carbonised receipt book in there was for, and I'd left it there pending further investigation. Now I knew.

I wrote up a chitty for the old couple and pulled a five-pound note from the till to pay them, but after accepting the slip of paper, Mrs Jorkins snatched her hand away.

'No, no, don't give me the money yet, my dear. Not till our goods have been sold. That's how Nell Little always managed things.'

'Well, if it's good enough for Nell Little, it's good enough for me,' I replied, exhaling a little puff of relief.

'By the way, if you don't mind my saying so, my dear, you've done the place up a treat,' said Mrs Jorkins, pocketing the receipt. 'If only Nell Little could see it, she'd be proud of you.'

Then she and her husband turned to go, making way for my next customer, without stopping to buy anything or even to browse the shop themselves.

16

THE INADVERTENT FAVOUR

'So, it seems that stuck-up Mrs Lawrence inadvertently did me a favour by showing me how Nell Little worked,' I explained to Danny, when at just after midday we were standing in an empty shop.

Well, I say empty. It was much fuller, stock-wise, than when I'd opened the door that morning. I hadn't sold a thing. What I'd taken for an eager queue of shoppers was merely an over-supply of suppliers. It seemed the villagers had been hoarding their unwanted items until the moment the Cotswold Curiosity Shop reopened for business. No wonder they'd been opposed to Terence Bolt's change-of-use application. They didn't want to lose the opportunity to dispose of their unwanted goods at a profit. When Maudie Frampton had told me the shop was a nice little earner, I had assumed she meant for me. I couldn't have been more wrong.

'Why don't they do what any normal twenty-first-century person would do and bung their stuff on eBay if they want to make money from it?' queried Danny. 'Or else donate it to a charity shop. Actually, I'd have thought a close-knit community like this would have its own market page on Facebook or WhatsApp.'

I shrugged. 'Search me. Perhaps old habits die hard, and Nell Little had been providing her service since before the internet was invented. Besides, the internet's not the answer to everything.'

'No, but it might solve a pressing problem for you now.'

I pulled out the stool tucked under the counter and slumped down onto it. It was the first time I'd sat down since I'd opened the shop.

Danny headed for a small, moss-green Lloyd Loom nursing chair and removed a creamy lace scatter cushion to make room for his bottom, which was rather broader than the dainty chair's intended user.

'Which particular problem do you have in mind?' I asked, leaning my elbows on the counter. 'Cajoling the despicable Glen to write me a reference that won't deter future employers from taking me on? Persuading a judge to let me keep my driving licence? Still no court date yet, by the way. I know the court system is really slow, but I hate being kept on tenterhooks. I'm not sure I should drive in the meantime, even once you've got my car fixed, in case a pending conviction might invalidate my insurance.'

'Nope, the internet can't help you with any of those,' he said calmly. 'But if you start listing your stock online, you'll probably get better prices and certainly more eyes on it than from passing trade in your shop. You can put any clothes and jewellery on specialist vintage clothing sites. They're bang on trend, you know, especially among young people, as well as environmentalists and the slow-fashion brigade.'

That was the one piece of Miles Swansong's advice that stood up to scrutiny. Danny's endorsement made me feel like one of those cartoon characters with pound signs in their eyes.

'Now I think of it, half of Steven's junk came from eBay in the first place. Sometimes the online auctions were really competitive so it makes sense for me to dispose of stuff that way too. If I'm here in the shop all day, I could probably fit the necessary admin into my working day while I'm waiting for customers to come in.'

I moved a few bits and pieces along the counter to clear a theoretical space for my laptop and jumped down from my stool.

'Look, the shop counter is the perfect height for a standing desk. How on trend am I now? Oh, Danny, suddenly this feels like it was meant to be!'

I grinned at him, genuinely inspired, and he smiled back, as if pleased to see me so happy. What a true friend he was. I was missing seeing him at the museum every day, but I was sure we'd stay close. He'd also be a useful contact when I wanted a second opinion on antique stock rather than bric-a-brac.

'How about we celebrate your first successful morning's trading with a coffee?' Danny suggested. 'If you make it, I'll hold the fort for you. If there's a sudden rush, I'll give you a shout.'

I thought 'successful' was a bit euphemistic, but I didn't disagree.

'Deal,' I said.

I returned a few minutes later with two ditsy, floral, bone-china cups and saucers, filled with fragrant espressos. Before we'd taken our first sip, the shop door creaked open, and a middle-aged couple dressed in walking gear staggered in. I'd noticed almost as soon as I'd moved in that a lot of walkers passed through the village, which was just off the Cotswold Way, the hugely popular National Trail that runs along the Cotswold Edge escarpment from Cheltenham in the north to Bath in the south.

'Please tell me you do hot drinks,' pleaded the woman, sinking down into the Lloyd Loom chair. There was far more room for her slender form, even with her backpack still on.

'Of course,' I said brightly. To be honest, it hadn't occurred to me to do so, but the poor soul looked exhausted. 'How do you take it?'

'It's £3 per cup, by the way,' added Danny. 'And it's served in beautiful mid-century china.'

He held up his cup and saucer, sprigged with forget-me-nots, to demonstrate.

'Or free if you make a purchase from the shop,' I added quickly, remembering from when we first opened the café at the museum that we had first to register our intention with the local authority and submit a food hygiene plan before it could trade. Not wanting to contravene regulations before the café was even officially open, I assumed giving away a coffee would be OK.

'Ooh, what a treat!' said the woman. She stretched out her legs and leaned down to massage her calves. 'I'm sure I can find something here to buy as a souvenir of our walk. In the meantime, can we please have two Americanos, one sugar, with a splash of milk.'

'I don't suppose you have any biscuits or cakes?' asked her husband, looking hopefully along the counter. 'We've already eaten everything we brought with us.'

I tapped the space I'd just cleared for my laptop. 'I was just about to fetch a fresh supply.'

I grabbed a sugar-pink cake stand from a shelf behind the counter and headed for the kitchen.

'There you go,' murmured Danny as I passed behind him. 'There's another string to your bow – or rather, another column to the income side of your ledger.'

'Once I've made it official, anyway. But great idea, Danny, thanks.'

I headed for the kitchen to produce from my cake tin a Victoria sponge I'd bought from Suki's Stores the day before and set it on the cake stand.

'Doilies,' I said to Danny as I came to stand behind him at the counter. 'Remind me to buy some paper doilies to add a vintage touch.'

'You've a basket of lace ones on the side table over there,' Danny observed. 'And plenty more vintage china.'

I was feeling increasingly grateful to Nell Little. It was almost as if she'd set this up for me.

'You could put a few patio tables and chairs on the hardstanding in front of the shop and call it a tea terrace,' said Danny. 'I noticed you've got some old bits of garden furniture out the back that you could repurpose. They just need sprucing up. After we've finished our coffee, I'll do that for you if you like. Then passers-by will stop for coffee and end up buying stuff from the shop on impulse. Double whammy.'

'Especially if I put a sign up saying "please order and pay at the counter",' I added, entering into the spirit of the thing. 'Then they'll have to wade past all the stock not once but twice. If they're the sort of people who enjoy tea at a place like this, they'll probably be the types to fill their homes with vintage household goods.'

'Cottagecore,' added Danny. 'That's got to be big in an area like this, and popular with the sort of tourists who visit here. Make sure you use it as a keyword in your website. You really ought to have a shop website. Nell Little didn't. I've been searching online for her, but all I can find is stuff about Charles Dickens.'

'My goodness, I'm going to be busy. When am I going to find time for job-hunting?'

Danny knew me far too well – better, I now realised, than Steven had ever done.

'You'll make time,' he replied. 'That is, if you want to.'

17

A TRICKY CUSTOMER

I was so buoyed up by Danny's series of brainwaves that when the next customer arrived, I half-expected him to be a fairy godfather who'd buy up half my stock and leave me with a stonking profit at the end of my first day's trading. I couldn't have been more wrong. The minute he crossed the threshold, the wiry little man's surly expression, thin lips twisted beneath a crooked nose, alerted me to trouble.

Although this visitor was shorter than me, I couldn't help wishing Danny was still in the shop, rather than scrubbing patio furniture in my back garden. Despite his diminutive stature, the stranger exuded menace. He halted in the middle of the shop floor, arms folded tightly across his chest, and surveyed my stock as if looking to find fault. Then he pointed to a corner where an old-fashioned tapestry draught excluder lay on the floor.

'Trip hazard,' he snapped, pointing in an accusatory manner.

Oh no, I thought, my stomach starting to churn. *This must be someone from the council coming to inspect my premises for health and safety already. How did they know? I haven't even applied to register the café yet. Has someone snitched on me to them?*

'It's a draught excluder,' I asserted, refusing to be riled. 'It's meant to go on the floor.'

'What about health and safety?' He spat out the words like a curse. 'You won't last long if you don't comply with health and safety. Supposing someone tripped over it? They might fall against that glass-fronted cabinet and cut their flesh to smithereens.'

He sounded as if he'd relish such a gruesome spectacle. Then he jabbed a finger at the sign on the counter I'd just made to show the price list for refreshments.

'You got a food hygiene certificate for that? Nell Little never served tea and cake. What makes you think you're entitled?'

Rather than engage in an argument, I decided on a charm offensive.

'Thank you for asking, yes I do, a personal one gained in my previous job. And my application to register the shop's café with the council is currently all in hand. This notice is just to raise awareness in advance.'

I took the chalk pen from the shelf beneath the counter and added a flash saying *Coming Soon!* to the menu board.

I was glad to hear footsteps behind me: Danny to my rescue. He seemed to have been doing that a lot lately.

'Yes, Alice is right, it's all in perfectly good order, thank you,' he said firmly, lifting the flap in the counter so he could get closer to the customer. He towered over the little man, who took a step back. 'I'm sorry, are you some kind of inspector from the council?'

The man stood a little taller, though still dwarfed by Danny.

'Not as such,' he replied. 'But the council and me – we're like that, see.' He held up crossed fingers. 'They set great store by my opinion at the council. I'm a leading local developer, see. Building as fast as I can to get all those new houses built to meet their target. Can't get enough of me, the council can't.'

'What, you mean you're building council houses on the

paddock?' said Danny. 'Rental homes for the local authority to run? How refreshing. There are not enough of those, for sure.'

The man rolled his eyes. 'Not me. I'm at the classy end of the market. Class and style, that's where the money is. See those new executive homes the other side of the pub?'

We couldn't, of course. The pub was at the far end of the high street.

'I built them, see. I'd have covered the allotments beside them too, if they'd let me.'

Not long after I'd moved in, I'd noticed the allotments next to the pub on an exploratory stroll around the village. They were idyllic, every inch expertly cultivated, and, like Coralie's plot, crammed with well-tended fruit and vegetables.

'Still working on that one,' he added. 'I expect I'll get it through on appeal. I usually do.'

I wondered how the allotment holders would feel about that.

'The paddock next door.' He jerked his thumb towards the donkey field. 'That was a walkover. Nasty nuisance, donkeys are, making such a racket.'

I sprang to their defence. 'I loved those donkeys, and I was very sorry to see them gone by the time I moved in.'

He tutted. 'Don't worry, you'll still have one next door.'

He jabbed his grubby thumb in the opposite direction to the paddock, indicating the house with the high boundary wall.

'Really? I haven't heard it braying yet. I suppose that high wall might be muffling the sound.'

The shop door creaked again, and this time a tall, slender man with slicked-back, steel-grey hair wandered in, gave a wave of greeting and a cheery 'Good afternoon', and began to browse the shop. The developer tutted again.

'Talk of the devil.'

The wiry little man pulled a dog-eared business card from hi pocket and slapped it down on the counter. It confirmed what I'd already guessed. This was the dreaded Terence Bolt that Coralie had warned me about, and Suki. Nutty Bolt, she'd called him.

'Anyway,' he continued, 'when you've had enough of playing shops here and can't make ends meet, I'll do you a favour and take the property off your hands. Leave it to me to name my price, mind. I know the market better than you will, see. No doubt that'll be before I've finished putting up my suite of new executive homes on your precious paddock. Paddock Close, it'll be now. That'll lure in more townies. They like countryfied addresses, like Paddock Close and Quarry Drive. Makes 'em think they're preserving the local heritage, like the National Trust or something.'

'When really they're trampling all over it,' murmured the man with the slicked-back hair, turning to me and winking.

I flushed with guilt at having planned to rename Nell's old home Curiosity Cottage, when it had always gone by the shop's name before.

When Bolt continued, unabashed, I wondered if he was a little deaf. It wouldn't have surprised me, given that he must have worked with noisy machinery for many years.

'In the meantime, I'll thank you not to get into any funny business with my workmen. Barnaby doesn't think I saw him creeping in here earlier with a box full of his pesky findings. But let me tell you, he had no right to flog them to you, see, and I want you to give them back to me right now. I'll be on to the boy like a ton of bricks for stealing my property.'

I hoped he was speaking metaphorically. He must have had at least a ton of bricks on the pallets in the paddock, ready to start building the houses.

I heaved the box of old bottles out from where I'd stashed them near the kitchen door and deposited it on the counter.

'By all means,' I said sweetly. 'Just on your way to the bottle bank, are you?'

Bolt tilted the box towards himself for a better look and gave it a shake, as if expecting something more valuable to rise to the surface.

'Oh, well, if tatty old glass is all it was, you're welcome to it. It's of no value to me.'

Then, like a dog having just marked its territory, he seemed spent. Turning on his heel, he headed for the door without more ado. As he pushed past the newcomer on his way out, the two men exchanged the sparsest of greetings, tight-lipped.

'Bolt.'

'Sponge.'

I couldn't help thinking that whatever awful thing had been the death of Nell Little, Terence Bolt might have had a part in it.

18

THE ETERNAL SPONGE

The suave newcomer's presence calmed me down after Bolt's departure. As he approached the counter, his broad, open smile revealed flawless white teeth suspiciously perfect for a man who looked a little older than me.

When Bob Sponge offered his hand to shake, I noticed his artistic, long fingers and neat, regular palms. It was the hand of a creative person. Perhaps he was a musician?

'Hello, I'm Robert,' he said with disarming simplicity. 'I'm your boy next door.'

I couldn't help but laugh at this gentle bit of flirting. Since Steven had left, I hadn't really thought about getting back out there, romance-wise. Although there had been the odd moment after his departure when I thought someone was chatting me up, but I'd chosen to ignore them. Now the twinkle in this gentle man's dark-brown eyes sent a spark of electricity through me that none of the others had produced. He had a good handshake, too – firm without being aggressive, and perfectly timed, combining confidence with respect. I felt as if someone had just applied jump leads to my inner battery.

'I'm Alice,' I replied. 'But you probably know that already. I'm glad to discover that I've got at least one nice next-door neighbour.'

'I'm so sorry. Has Terence Bolt been giving you a hard time? I'm afraid he hasn't yet forgiven you for buying a property he wanted.'

'If he wanted it so much, why didn't he simply outbid me? I got it for a song compared to the house I was selling in town. I'm glad he didn't, by the way.'

Robert shrugged. 'Because he's a terrible businessman with a permanent cash-flow crisis. But between you and me, I'm glad he didn't, because he'd have just ripped out all the period features to match his new-builds. That's one of my passions, by the way – preserving old residential properties, complete with their original features, while seamlessly adding modern conveniences and energy efficiency.'

I wondered what his other passions were.

'That's why I bought the house next door,' he added. 'I'm a serial restorer of old houses. This is my seventeenth. Think of me as the antidote to the Terence Bolts of this world. I restore them to a high standard, then rent them out. There's always a shortage of rental properties in rural communities, and few are purpose-built these days. All the new-builds are so-called executive homes like the preposterous monstrosities Terence Bolt is building. Well, they don't appeal to this executive, I can tell you.'

Now he'd sparked the business part of my brain. If he was into vintage homes, he might like what I was selling in my shop, and if he was a monied executive of some kind, he wouldn't be short of cash. The housing restoration projects were probably just a hobby.

'So, do you work locally or commute into town?'

I was trying not to race ahead, but if I was about to lose my driving licence and found another city-based job, lift-sharing with Robert would be no hardship for me.

He narrowed his eyes in contemplation of what I thought was a very simple question.

'My head office is in Singapore,' he replied at last. 'But I only travel there once a month, staying for a week at a time. Otherwise, I'm nomadic, paying spot visits to my various plants in the UK and Europe, but Little Pride is where I call home.'

'So, you're in agriculture?'

I wondered what kind of plants might grow equally well in both Singapore and Europe.

He let out a hearty laugh. 'Not that kind of plant, although plants of the photosynthesising variety are the main components of my key product. Here, let me demonstrate.'

He delved into the side pocket of his perfectly fitting, black Levis and produced a flat, lime-green object shaped like an oak leaf. He set it on the palm of his hand, held it out to show me, then curled his fingers around it. It looked a comfortable fit.

'It expands when you put it in water, but the two-dimensional quality when dry makes shipping very economical. You may have heard of it? It's called the Eternal Sponge. It's an everlasting wash-ing-up sponge, totally environmentally friendly, carbon neutral, soft on the hands and needing no detergent. Buy one of these, and you'll never need another, nor any other kind of washing-up acces-sory. Safe on non-stick, tough on baked-on scraps. No artificial chemicals involved or required.'

Of course, like everyone else, I'd heard of the Eternal Sponge, although I didn't want to admit to Robert that I'd never sufficiently trusted the advertising hype to invest the thirty-pound price tag.

'Gosh, I never realised you'd named the Eternal Sponge after yourself.' I smiled. 'What a striking example of nominative deter-minism. That's like me being called Alice Bric-a-Brac.'

He frowned in mock seriousness. 'So, are you one of the Hamp-shire Bric-a-Bracs?'

I laughed. 'I wish. My real surname is Carroll. And before you ask, as everybody else does, yes, my mum was a lifelong *Alice in Wonderland* fan, though no relation to her author. Hence my first name. But enough about me. Sponge is such an unusual surname. I've only ever come across two other people called Sponge, and neither were real. One was the cartoon character, and the other a minor character in the television series *Dad's Army* – Private Sponge.'

'I'm quite a private person too.' He held my gaze in a way that made me feel positively exposed. 'But Sponge isn't my real name either. It's just the daft nickname the locals have chosen to give me after my most successful product. I just hope the planning brigade at the local council haven't heard about it. They feel a bit threatened by me, as I'm a stickler for detail and I'm not afraid of calling them out. I've given Terence Bolt a few frights by picking holes in his planning applications. He's forever trying to cut costs on his new-builds, so I get my architects to check out every one of his applications and file objections whenever they find things wanting. Not that it does much good in the long term. Bolt usually gets his plans passed on appeal. But it's partly my objections that scuppered his change-of-use application for the Cotswold Curiosity Shop. Long story short, anyone prepared to keep the shop trading was able to buy it for a bargain price. I'm glad that anyone turned out to be you.'

This intelligence unnerved me slightly. I hoped he wasn't looking for favours in return.

'To be honest, I'm surprised the national media haven't picked up on the Bob Sponge gag yet either,' he continued. 'They'd have a field day with punning headlines. They like to have a pop at me whenever they can. The British press doesn't like a self-made billionaire industrialist who rose from the ranks of a state education.'

'Gosh, I'm impressed! Fancy selling enough washing-up sponges to make you a billionaire, especially when I gather they're a once-in-a-lifetime purchase.'

Robert gave a modest smile. 'Oh, we've other products too – a sponge for all occasions, not just the Eternal Sponge for kitchens. Bigger ones for bathtubs and floors, even bigger ones for washing cars, plus, at the other end of the spectrum, tiny make-up applicators. All available to buy worldwide from my company website if you can't find them in your local shops.'

My shoulders slumped in disappointment. Here I was, thinking he was chatting me up. Really, he was just a glorified door-to-door salesman, an upmarket version of the Betterware man that used to visit my gran with his sample case of lavender polishes and yellow dusters. Perhaps his fortune came from pyramid selling. If he tried to recruit me, I'd give him short shrift. I wasn't that desperate for work.

'Here, have this one on me,' he said. He took my hand and pressed his free sample sponge into my palm. I hoped this wasn't a modern equivalent of taking the King's shilling, obliging me to evangelise for his products for ever more.

Even so, as a housework enthusiast, I was keen to try the Eternal Sponge. With the rest of the cottage to spring-clean now that I'd brought the shop up to scratch, I'd have the perfect testing ground for his claim that his Eternal Sponge was indestructible.

Perhaps he detected my slight discomfort at the change of tone in the conversation, because he stepped back from the counter and turned to gaze around the shop.

'Now on to what I really came in for,' he said lightly. 'I've been waiting for your shop to reopen to I could nab those gorgeous stone storage jars over there.'

He went to the far corner of the shop to collect the set of six heavy, biscuit-coloured glazed pots. I'd washed them a few days before and remembered each one weighed a ton. He brought them two at a time to the counter.

'Perfect for my restored larder next door,' he explained, reaching into the back pocket of his jeans. He pulled out his phone and opened a payment app, then looked around for an electronic payment device. That flustered me.

'I'm sorry, I'm not set up for card payments yet. The machine's on order.'

That was a lie, but mentally I added ordering a card machine to my to-do list.

'No worries, Alice,' he replied, returning the phone to his pocket and pulling out a wad of banknotes instead. He counted out three twenty-pound notes, each one as crisp and crease-free as if newly minted, and placed them side by side on the counter. 'I assume cash is acceptable? If not, I can come back once you've got your card payment system set up. Just shout over the garden wall whenever you want me, and I'll come running.'

He gave a cheeky wink, and I blushed slightly.

Just then, a clattering sound came from the back room, and Danny appeared, carrying a spotless round patio table, the wet wood darkened where he'd given it a thorough wash.

Catching the flirtatious flavour of the conversation, Danny glanced quizzically from Robert to me and back again. Robert flashed him a winning smile.

'Oh, hello. I didn't realise Alice had a partner in crime.'

'He's not...' I began to say but thought better of it. Maybe it was sensible to allow Robert to think Danny and I were an item, whether in terms of business or romance. It would have been too easy to be swayed by this charming billionaire, but I was on my guard. I was bound to be vulnerable so soon after Steven's departure.

Danny set down the patio table and lifted the counter flap, his eye on the stoneware jars. He picked up two in each hand. 'Here, let me help you with these to your car.'

Who was he trying to impress most: me with his helpfulness or Robert with his physical strength? Or was he just trying to get rid of Robert?

'Do you have your car outside, Mr...?'

'Praed,' replied Robert. 'Yes, like the famous actor, but no relation. Actually, it's an old village name.'

'So, you're one of the Gloucestershire Praeds?' I quipped, then felt bad for excluding Danny from our earlier private joke about the Hampshire Bric-a-Bracs.

Robert smiled, reminding me of his expensive teeth. I wondered whether he'd had anything else enhanced.

'I suppose so. Although there have been umpteen spellings of our family name over the centuries. There are at least four versions on the village war memorial and in the churchyard.'

'So, you are local, then,' I said. 'Not just an incomer like me.'

He nodded as he picked up the remaining two jars. 'Yes, my heart belongs to Little Pride, and so do my genes. However far I travel, for business or pleasure, I always return here. I'm the proverbial bad penny. That's why I was so glad to snap up my boyhood home next door when it came back on the market a few years ago. Thankfully, that was before Little Pride was on our friend Terence Bolt's radar.'

'Was the high boundary wall there when you were a child, or did you build it to retain your privacy?'

Now that I knew he was a wealthy celebrity in industrial circles, I could understand if he felt a need for security to fend off paparazzi and the like.

'Oh yes, it's decades old. My great-grandfather was passionate about espaliering fruit trees, so he had it built. A passionate lot, my forebears.'

I gave a foolish grin. Then Danny coughed and asked Robert where his car was again.

'I came on foot, all the way from next door,' replied Robert, nodding in the direction of his house.

I admit I had rather warmed to Robert Praed, but when Danny followed him out of the shop, I could tell from Danny's demeanour that he didn't feel the same.

'Too smooth by half,' he murmured on his return.

As soon as he'd spoken, I felt foolish for being so gullible. Surely no one could really make billions from selling washing-up sponges? Perhaps there was another reason behind his village nickname. Maybe he had a reputation as a parasite.

Suddenly, I was no longer sure which of my new neighbours, if any, I could trust.

19

CORRALLING CORALIE

After Robert Praed's departure, sales began to pick up, with quite a few tourists calling in during the afternoon. A few villagers also returned, this time to browse my displays and buy things, rather than bringing more stock. By the end of my opening day, the shop felt considerably more cluttered than it had at the start, thanks to several hundred pounds worth of stock acquired from villagers. I was relieved that Nell Little had reserved the right to return to their original owners any items unsold within three months.

Better news was that I'd taken £257 in sales. Although I couldn't expect such high takings every day, I was glad to be so well supported on my first day of trading. Even old Maudie Frampton bought an old felt hat for a fiver, although she froze when Danny appeared from the back parlour bringing me a coffee, clearly recognising him as the man she'd taken for a squatter. I distracted her by smiling sweetly and telling her how much the hat suited her.

I was glad to see Andrew Gloster again mid-afternoon, when he kindly returned with his camera to take a photo of me behind the counter for the next edition of the *Little Pride Parish News*. At my request, he took another picture with Danny on what I had grandly christened the tea terrace, which was now adorned with the wooden tables and chairs that Danny had hosed down. Andrew generously offered to email me the images so that I could send them to the local paper, in hope of drawing in some customers from further afield. Proudly, he told me the local paper often picked up stories from the *Little Pride Parish News*.

'Don't forget, you'll need photos for your website too,' said Danny.

When I asked Andrew if he'd like to be in a photo with me, so that I could publicly acknowledge his support, he quickly declined.

'I prefer to keep a low profile, thank you,' he said, sidling out of the door before I could argue.

Could what Suki told me about him being a spy really be true? Maybe he had retired to Little Pride from the international espionage circuit. He might even be living under an assumed identity in a safe house. As safe houses go, the Big House must have been top of the range, judging by what I'd seen of it when I dropped my note off to him. It was not just big, but huge: a double-fronted, three-storey Elizabethan mansion tucked behind high walls. The gravelled forecourt was big enough to allow cars – and presumably once carriages – to turn around the ornamental fountain in front of the house.

I supposed spies must get generous pensions, if they survive long enough to draw them. Perhaps that was one reason he took such pride in his position as editor of the parish magazine – it was an absurdly cosy position after a career that required him to put his life on the line.

Of the other friends I'd already made in the village, I wasn't surprised that Suki didn't come to my opening day, as she'd have been at work in her own shop. Coralie, too, was most likely in her salon. But when she still hadn't collected the glass vases she'd asked for, despite the card I'd left for her, I decided on the Sunday to venture round to her tiny house behind Coralie's Curls and deliver them to her.

After spending so much time in my shop, I was ready for a change of scene, and for more orderly surroundings than the rest of my cottage, still a cluttered cocktail of my possessions and Nell's leavings.

So, at three o'clock in the afternoon, I headed for Strumpet's Patch, passing several people I'd recognised as my previous day's customers. They all gave me a friendly hello. I was starting to feel as if I belonged.

Coralie was sitting on the steps of her shepherd's hut, reading a book.

'So, how did yesterday go?' she cried as soon as she saw me.

She stood up and beckoned me inside. I half expected to find myself in some kind of TARDIS, much bigger inside than out. Absurdly, I was more surprised to find it the same size as it looked from its exterior: tiny indeed. Like her salon, it was adorned with an eclectic mix of hand-made soft furnishings and dried flowers.

From a stone cider jar with a metal tap set into the side, she poured us a fragrant opaque drink the colour of dishwater but with the scent of a summer's day. I sniffed it tentatively, wondering about the alcohol content. I'd been on the wagon since the unnerving experience of losing my memory at the redundancy drinks.

'Don't worry, it won't kill you,' she assured me. 'It's only my home-made ginger beer. Perfectly harmless.'

We both settled down on an old double bus seat. The original prickly velour was covered with faded ticking in stripes of duck-egg blue and egg-yolk yellow. I was halfway through my drink before I remembered her vases. When I produced them from my tote bag, her face lit up. I was glad to be able to bring her so much pleasure with something from my shop.

'So, spill the beans. How was your grand reopening?' She settled back into the corner of the bus seat, crossing her legs in the lotus position.

'It went far better than I expected, although at first I was taken aback at being asked to sell the villagers' things on their behalf,' I told her.

She put her hand to her mouth. 'Sorry, Alice, I should have thought to tell you about that arrangement. It's so NULPY.'

'So whatty?'

'NULPY.' She spelled out the initials. 'Not Unusual for Little Pride.'

I laughed.

'But don't worry,' she added. 'You'll be glad of the extra stock now the main tourist season is starting up. Lots of passers-by will call in as part of their tours of Cotswold attractions. You've got the place up and running again at exactly the right time. Well done you.'

'More by luck than judgement – and with a little help from my friends. Danny was a godsend yesterday, dispensing coffees, which boosted my takings nicely, and he cleaned the patio tables up a treat. I've put them all in front of the shop now, as a kind of café. It's no longer empty, bare hardstanding, but a tea terrace.'

I made air quotes, not wanting to sound pretentious, but Coralie seemed impressed.

'Fab. That'll encourage more people to stop by, and those who do will linger longer. But who's Danny? Your fella?'

'No, Danny's just Danny. My best mate from my old job, and a real friend in a crisis.'

'Is Danny going to be working at the shop too? It'll be tough to eke two salaries out of it, even in the height of the summer.'

'Goodness, no. Unlike me, he managed to hang on to his job at the museum when I lost mine. Although I admit having him on my staff would not be without its attractions. Anyway, tell me what you know about Robert Praed.'

'Bob Sponge? Oh, he's OK. Nice enough guy to have as your next-door neighbour, although he's not there much, what with his international wheeler-dealing and all the other houses he owns about the place. He's just got his bolthole here to escape from the pressures of his business, and for sentimental reasons, of course. Did you know his family goes back generations in the village?'

'Yes, he mentioned that.'

'Rumour has it, they were once very rich, before one of his fore-bears frittered a lot of the family fortune away in some gambling scandal. That's why they ended up selling his childhood home. Bob's really a self-made man. But if you look around the church-yard, you'll see loads of Praeds on the gravestones, and on the war memorial too. Not always spelled as he spells it, but then it's only in the last hundred years or so that we've had universal literacy, isn't it? So, you'll find Pridds, Prades and Prods, and even the odd Prada among them.'

I laughed. 'I don't suppose the famous fashion house would be pleased about that. Though I don't think you can trademark a person's name unless they use it for business. If Robert Praed was promoting his Eternal Sponge as the Prada Washing-up Sponge, that might be a different matter.'

'I suppose so. But Bob's OK. Like I told you the other day, it's your other neighbour, Terence Bolt, you need to keep an eye on.'

20

COMPOSTING DOWN

On the following day, I was rather hoping Barnaby would forget his lunch again, so that he'd call in to barter for his morning coffee. To be honest, I'd have given it to him for free, even if he had nothing to swap for it.

It was a gorgeous summer's day, and I decided to take my own elevenses out onto the terrace, where he'd doubtless see me if he was about. It would be a shame if Bolt's scolding had put him off visiting my shop again. I liked Barnaby and would have been happy to count him as a regular.

However, when I took my coffee out onto the terrace and chose a table with a good view of the paddock, Barnaby was nowhere to be seen, and nor was Bolt. The only person on site was Barnaby's colleague, digging with a gleaming spade in the patch where the stable used to be. I waved to get his attention. Scowling at being interrupted, he raised his spade and rested it on his shoulder before trudging over to talk to me.

'Hi there, is Barnaby about, please?'

I raised my voice when I spoke my friend's name, thinking it might lure him out from wherever he might be lurking on site.

'Barnaby?' The labourer spat out the name. 'What's wrong with me? I'm Magnus. Why does everyone always want Barnaby? Anyway, you're out of luck. He's not here today. Off sick with food poisoning, Mr Bolt said, from the rubbish you've been feeding him at your illegal café. You'd better clean up your kitchen, Mr Bolt says, if you don't want the council shutting you down.'

'There's nothing wrong with my kitchen,' I retorted automatically, while racking my brains to think what the sell-by date had been on that packet of ham. If there was something wrong with it, it must have been in a big way, because it would take a lot to fell a hulk of a fellow like Barnaby. 'And besides, my café's not even operational yet.'

Magnus lowered his spade and sank the blade deep into the ground with a single thrust, making me realise his brute strength. He'd be more than a match for Barnaby. How I wished Danny was still around.

But my rescue came from a far less likely source.

'Coo-ee!' came a high-pitched woman's voice behind me. I turned round to find Maudie Frampton, beady eyes twinkling, as she looked from me to Magnus and back again.

She set down the ancient wheelbarrow full of gardening tools that she was pushing up the high street. They looked as if they'd already served several generations of her family.

'Poison, eh?' she cried with glee. 'Who's poisoned who? Shall I go and fetch the quack? I'll pass his house on the way to my allotment.'

'No, busybody,' snapped Magnus.

'No one's poisoned anybody, Maudie, don't worry,' I said quickly. The last thing I needed was for her to start putting word about the village that I'd been poisoning my customers.

Her shoulders sagged in disappointment. 'Then I'll be on my way.'

But if excitement was what she was looking for, she was heading in the right direction. Not long after I'd returned to my shop and Magnus to his digging, I heard the most awful shrieking coming from further up the high street. I ran out of my shop, letting the door slam behind me. I raced down the path and gazed in the direction of the screams.

There was Maudie Frampton, charging down the high street as fast as her hobnailed boots would carry her, her barrow, now bereft of its load, freewheeling so fast that it was a wonder it didn't pull her off her feet.

Several neighbours had come out of their houses to see what the noise was about, but Maudie ran past them, stopping only when she reached my terrace.

Wheezing, she slumped down onto one of my terrace chairs, and I stooped to clasp her wizened, muddy hands in reassurance.

'Maudie, whatever's the matter? What's wrong?'

I couldn't begin to imagine what in Little Pride could have so spooked this sturdy old soul. Her fear was infectious, and I was beginning to feel quite shaky myself as she pointed back up the high street, wide-eyed.

'My allotment!' she gasped, struggling to the words out. 'Terrible trouble at my allotment.'

I relaxed. No doubt it was just a gardening issue rather than mortal danger. Perhaps a jealous rival had sabotaged the prize marrow she'd been raising for the village show, or some naughty children had been scrumping in her soft fruit bed.

'Deep, slow breaths, Maudie,' I counselled, experienced at dealing with minor crises and the occasional panic attack among museum visitors. 'I'm sure whatever it is, you'll feel better once you've had a nice cup of hot, sweet tea.'

I looked around for someone either to take the hint and fetch her one, or to take over from me while I did, but everyone was keeping their distance.

Maudie drew back her shoulders and pulled her hands away from mine.

'Alice Carroll,' she scolded. Her tone instantly told me she'd once been a schoolteacher, many years before. 'I like a nice cup of tea as much as the next person but even the tastiest brew in the world isn't going to bring a dead body back to life.'

I wondered whether whatever had shocked her had sent her temporarily insane. I laid two fingers gently on the pulse point of her right wrist and smiled.

'Look, you're far from being a dead body. I can feel your heart ticking away as soundly as the church tower clock.'

Maudie snatched her scrawny wrist away as if I'd just sunk my teeth into it.

'Not me, mutton-head!' she exclaimed, with a withering look. 'I'm talking about the dead builder in my compost heap!'

21

THE CIRCLE OF LIFE

Poor Barnaby. He was such a nice chap. I couldn't imagine that anyone would have anything against him, apart from Bolt and Magnus, of course. But I was wary of making such a serious accusation against Bolt for such a minor offence as donating what he considered unwanted rubbish to the Cotswold Curiosity Shop or against Magnus for jealousy. Besides, although I knew Bolt was cross with Barnaby for giving me stuff he'd dug up on his paddock, he hadn't seemed exactly in a murderous rage about it.

I pulled another tissue from the box on my dining table as Andrew, who had been one of the crowd who turned out at Maudie's screams, poured me a cup of strong tea. Maudie had already been escorted home by her daughter, who looked of pensionable age herself, and the crowd that had assembled outside my shop had quickly dispersed when it became clear that the centre of the action – or rather, of Barnaby's extreme inaction – was at the allotments.

'I can't believe anyone would want to kill him, Andrew.' I sniffed. 'And certainly Maudie Frampton couldn't have been his assailant. Although she's undeniably tough for her age, he was twice her size and about a quarter of her age.'

'No, she's just unlucky that his killer chose her allotment as their hiding place.'

Remembering my reputation as being the museum sleuth, I was keen to contribute my skills to solving the mystery.

'Whereabouts is Maudie's allotment?' I asked.

'On the plot beyond the pub, same as everybody else's,' he answered, before getting up and turning his back to me to search my cupboards for the biscuit tin.

'No, I mean where exactly within the plot of land that makes up all the allotments.'

He grunted as he wrenched the lid off the tin. 'At the back, I think, by the wall.'

I waved away his offer of a biscuit. 'Which gives on to open fields, I think?'

He nodded. 'Yes. Does that matter?'

I took a sip of tea while I rehearsed my theory in my head. 'Yes, because it means someone could easily have carried the body round from wherever Barnaby was murdered and heaved it over the wall onto the closest allotment. That would make it less likely they'd be seen, especially if they were doing it in the dead of night. Sorry, unfortunate choice of words.'

Andrew finished eating a shortbread finger before replying. 'Yes, but why would anyone hide a body on the allotments? Daft place to choose if you ask me, because it'll have the most densely planted soil in the village. Apart from the building site of course.'

I raised a finger, as if asserting my authority. 'Ah, but maybe it was meant to be a temporary resting place before they could recover it and take the body wherever they planned to make its final destination.'

I felt slightly sick talking about 'the body' as if it was a random stranger, when it was someone I knew personally and liked very much.

'And the smell of the compost would mask the – the smell of the body,' I continued, gulping.

Andrew sighed. 'You townie, Alice! It's obvious you've never built a compost heap. When it's done properly, they don't smell at all. That's just an urban myth.'

He was right.

'OK, but even so, if you surrounded a rotting body' – I was so glad I hadn't had that biscuit – 'with enough compost, it'll mask any smell of decay simply by its bulk.'

Andrew narrowed his eyes at me. 'You don't miss much, do you?'

I smiled, pleased at his compliment. After all, if he really was a spy, he should have made a better detective than me.

'But wouldn't someone on the high street have spotted them hiding the body there?' he queried.

'Not if they did it after dark,' I said. 'I mean after the streetlights have been turned off at midnight. And if they delivered the body from the field, rather than from the road.'

'Yes,' said Andrew. 'And although the houses either side of the allotments have security lights, I've noticed they're only in the front. I bet they'll soon be adding more to their back gardens after this.'

I was starting to think more clearly now, the adrenaline rush caused by Maudie's shocking news sending me into fight mode.

'Even so,' I added, 'although there's not much that goes on in the high street that isn't witnessed by someone, if you picked your moment, and kept your eye out for any passers-by, you could probably get away with it.'

Andrew helped himself to a Bourbon. 'Although it might be that they did plan to bury him there, but were townies themselves, and didn't realise how well cultivated the plots would be. As I'm sure you've seen, Alice, every inch of soil is raising some fruit or vegetable at this time of year. Which makes me think it was a country person, a villager, who killed him, as they chose not to destroy the crops. They'd be only too aware how upsetting it would be to have your prizewinning gladioli or heritage beans disturbed.'

I had to wonder about their priorities.

'Or perhaps they were going to bury it and replace the crops on top, until they were disturbed by a late-night dog-walker,' I suggested. 'Or by someone leaving the pub after a lock-in, and they had to improvise with the compost heap and flee.'

Andrew frowned. 'Or else it was someone trying to frame poor old Maudie, someone with a grudge against her.'

He glanced at me for my reaction, then looked away quickly, but not before I noticed his accusatory expression.

I edged my chair back a little. 'Surely you don't mean me, Andrew? I know I didn't get off to the best of starts with her, but do you really think I'm strong enough to kill a man and lug his body across the fields from my back garden to the allotments, just to get my own back on her for the rude comments she made about me and Danny?'

Andrew's laugh sounded forced to me. 'Sorry, Alice, I'm just playing devil's advocate. Old habit from a former life. Anyway, we can speculate all we like, but the crime is in the hands of the police now.'

He picked up his empty cup and saucer and took them to the sink to wash up.

'I daresay the police will be questioning us all for evidence in due course,' he remarked. 'If, when your turn comes, you want a friend there for moral support, just give me a bell.'

I stared into my cup, swirling the remains around as if hoping to find the answer to the mystery in the tea leaves.

'Thank you, Andrew, that's very kind of you,' I said quietly.

But if and when the police came to question me, I wanted to be able to speak to them in confidence. I wasn't entirely sure I could trust Andrew more than any other of my neighbours.

22

THE COACH PARTY

By the following Monday, there was still no conviction for Barnaby's murder, despite an intensive programme of police questioning. Maudie, who had been taken to the police station on the day she discovered the body, was sent home in a police car a few hours later with no charges against her. Detectives also visited every house in the village at least once. Maudie's gardening tools, however, had been impounded for forensic testing – as had her entire compost heap.

To the horror of allotment holders, all the plots were still sealed off by crime-scene tape, and a small, white tent erected on the gravel path housed the scenes of crime officers as they searched the area for evidence. No one was allowed even to water their plot, to the detriment of their produce in this warm July week. Maudie, rallying remarkably quickly after her ordeal, put it about the village that the police were secretly using their tent to picnic on the allotment crops.

Bolt, meanwhile, kept a low profile, and he looked thinner and gaunter every time I saw him. Now down to a single labourer, the pressure of time on him to complete and sell the new executive homes before his loans were called in must have been unbearable. Surely it would have made more sense to hire more workers to get the job done faster, but maybe he'd simply run out of funds – or of lenders to tide him over. If he wasn't careful, he'd end up physically ill as well as stressed.

It took a great deal of resolve to rise above the constant gossip about the mystery and focus instead on the running of my shop. However, I was grateful to have the distraction to stop me over-thinking what had happened to poor Barnaby.

I tried hard to lay down a rigid routine to govern my day. Having breakfast by 9 a.m. on my back garden patio before opening the shop at ten in theory gave me an hour to concentrate on job applications before I would be disturbed by any customers. Although there was so much admin to do for the shop – from setting up the website and adding stock to eBay, to writing to the local paper and penning my article for the next issue of the *Little Pride Parish News* – I wasn't managing to fit in much job-hunting.

Taking my breakfast out into the back garden gave me the opportunity to do a little light industrial espionage on the building site next door. Work there started before I was awake each day. I was able to rely on the sounds of Bolt's machinery to serve as my alarm clock, at least until he'd finished excavating the foundations.

In the absence of Barnaby, there was now only Bolt and Magnus in the paddock. Both scowled whenever they saw me. Refusing to let them intimidate me, I continued my charm offensive, giving a friendly wave to the pair of them. I tried not to get too distracted, though. It was all very well being neighbourly, but I had a business to run.

* * *

After flicking a feather duster over my wares, I took a seat behind the counter and opened my laptop. I had plenty of admin to do before I opened up for the morning. Top of my list was to apply for a dropped kerb to fend off further criticism from fierce old Maudie Frampton and to register my proposed café with the local authority. Even though I was pleased with the tea terrace Danny and I had created, in the winter I might want to put the tables away and turn it into a parking space instead.

After clicking the submit button on the planning application, I stood up and stretched my neck and back. The sun streaming in through the shop window was making the atmosphere a little close, so I came out from behind the counter to prop the front door open with a large flat iron that had been adorning the larger pine dresser. *That's good psychology*, I told myself as I turned to straighten a display of hand-embroidered tablecloths. *An open doorway is far more enticing than a closed one, and may encourage waverers to come in.*

I should also put flowers on the café tables, I decided. I could even do that now, both to remind passers-by that I was breathing new life into Nell Little's shop, and as a private tribute to Barnaby's memory. I gathered a few of the larger bottles that Barnaby had brought me, now spotlessly clean. I set them on the counter, and filled them with wildflowers from my back garden.

Then, while looking for an empty box to use for paper recycling, I came across the second box of Barnaby's donations, which I hadn't shown to Bolt: the fragments of ceramics. I fetched the box from the cupboard and rifled through it. They looked pretty old to me – pre-Victorian, for sure, so not in my area of expertise. But even so, they didn't seem sufficiently valuable for Bolt or anyone else to kill Barnaby over.

Just as the alarm on my phone reminded me it was time to open up, the grinding of gears and a pungent waft of diesel from in front of the shop distracted my attention from the task in hand. So much for the open door filling the shop with fresh country air.

If the coach was bearing tourists keen to visit my shop, I'd forgive the driver for the fumes. I just hoped they weren't the gruesome kind who had come to gawp at the last places Barnaby had been seen. News of the murder had, not surprisingly, made the front page of the local paper.

Sure enough, as the passengers disembarked, they headed straight into the shop, their dark suits dour in the bright sunshine. Not what most tourists would choose to wear for a sunny day trip to the countryside, nor would they usually carry clipboards. A business team on a team-building exercise, perhaps, such as a treasure hunt with quiz sheets at the ready? That would explain the clipboards, but why the suits?

By the time I'd twigged they weren't tourists at all, but some kind of officials, the first of them had made his way to the counter. The rest began milling around the shop, chattering to each other in low voices, as if they didn't want me to hear.

'Good morning, Miss Carroll,' said their apparent leader, a sandy-haired chap of about forty, who, if he had a chin, must have left it on the bus. 'We're from the council's planning department, and we've come to make an investigative inspection with regard to the recent application pertaining to this property.'

'Blimey, that was quick,' I replied, genuinely astonished. 'I only submitted my applications for a dropped kerb and café a few minutes ago.'

He raised his eyebrows in puzzlement. 'Oh no, we're not here about that. If you've sent in a dropped kerb application today, we won't be able to process it for at least two months.'

'But I haven't sent in a previous application.' I was beginning to feel like my namesake at the Mad Hatter's tea party. 'I've only ever submitted the forms that I completed just now.'

He brightened. 'Ah, we're not here to process *your* application, Miss Carroll.'

'Then are you sure you're in the right place? I'm the sole proprietor of this shop and the owner of the cottage. Surely any application would have to come from me.'

His face clouded. 'This is the Cotswold Curiosity Shop, is it not? Unless my eyes deceive me?'

I pursed my lips. I'd had enough of self-important, pen-pushing men telling me what to do when I worked at the museum. I wasn't going to stand for it now I was my own boss.

'Yes, and I'm rather busy just now, so please tell me why you're here and be done with it,' I said firmly. Only after I'd spoken did I remember that it might not be smart to get on the wrong side of the council planners.

He cleared his throat and pulled himself up to his full height. He clearly wanted to make a show of whatever it was he had to say. I almost offered him a box to stand on.

'We're in receipt of a fresh application for change of use of this retail property with living accommodation, to purely residential, and we're here to consider its merits under the current circumstances.'

'An application from whom?'

'It's all on the planning application section of the council website if you take the trouble to look.'

When he tapped my laptop with the tip of his ballpoint pen, I felt as affronted as if he had jabbed me in the chest with it.

'But I was told you'd already refused the change of use, both an initial application from Mr Bolt the builder, and his appeal against your refusal.'

The planning officer allowed himself a smug smile. 'Ah, but the circumstances have changed. Those refusals were for when the site was situated next to the plot of land in agricultural use.'

'You mean the historic paddock.'

I noticed a couple of his colleagues smirking at my defiance. They must have found it tiresome to deal with this pompous windbag day in, day out. Every meeting with him must have taken twice as long as necessary. He continued, unperturbed.

'Yet now we are considering a property sandwiched between other residential properties. A further residential property would not seem so incongruous in the changed circumstances.'

So that was Bolt's game. He hadn't taken his sights off adding my cottage to his empire, even though it now belonged to me. Knowing how the council operated, and having allies in its midst, he was trying again, despite my house no longer being up for sale. I felt my colour rising at his arrogance. He really was willing my shop to fail so he could snap it up at a discounted price.

Well, that decided me. Perhaps I could beat him at his own game. If he was able to get change-of-use permission from the council for the shop, that change of use would apply to me too – and I could transform it into residential for my own use, without having to foot the bill for the application.

One way or another, there was no way I'd let that smug weasel get his paws on it, even if it meant I had to make a go of running it as a shop for the rest of my days.

At that moment, the crowd of council officers – presumably all connected with planning consent in some way – began to shuffle about, parting to leave a clear path in the middle of the shop floor. Strutting towards the counter between them was Terence Bolt himself, nodding to the visitors and giving a feeble impression of a royal wave as he passed them by. The murmurs from the crowd told me they were less eager to see him than he might have thought.

The reaction of the man at the counter was quite the opposite. When he spun on his heel to see the source of the disturbance, his face lit up, and his lips parted in a sickly smile, revealing yellowing teeth in bad repair.

'Terence Bolt!' he cried, thrusting his right hand out.

Bolt pumped the man's hand as if raising water from a well. 'Keith McCreedy, how the devil are you? Fancy seeing you here!'

At least I knew his name now. How rude he had been not to tell it to me himself, especially when he already knew mine. But this was no chance encounter. Bolt must have had a tip-off. They began a charade of praise for the shop, as if hoping to throw me off their scent.

'Hasn't Miss Carroll done well to reopen so soon after moving in?' Bolt was saying. He turned his back to me and began to show McCreedy around as if he owned the shop himself. 'Of course, this room hasn't always been a shop. It would originally have been a charming front parlour, and so it could be again, don't you agree?'

I lifted the counter flap and marched out to join them, the herd of council staff parting again to allow me through.

'You go, girl,' whispered a young woman with pink hair at odds with the conformity of her anonymous grey trouser suit.

'One moment, please, ladies and gentlemen.' I drew level with them beside a row of milk churns, ideal for repurposing as garden planters. 'What about the council's Shop Local campaign? I thought your stated mission was to keep local shops open at all costs, especially in rural communities whose residents may not have transport to access urban shopping centres?'

The weasel twins exchanged conspiratorial glances.

'It's all a question of balance,' said McCreedy. 'We protect local shops, of course, especially those that sell essentials to daily life, such as bread and milk and newspapers. But I question how critical your stock is to the daily survival of the villagers.'

He picked up a set of brass scales, marked in imperial measures. 'How often might one need to buy an object like this, for example?'

An older lady in his party raised her hand.

'I always cook in pounds and ounces,' she said.

I shot her a warm smile of appreciation, making a mental note of her appearance. If she ever returned as a customer, I'd give her a discount.

'Besides, there is a genuine need to redress the balance in favour of smaller homes in this area, and your property has just two bedrooms, I believe?' replied McCreedy. 'The ideal affordable starter home.'

'The balance is only out of kilter because you've allowed Mr Bolt to build a whole rash of very large properties in the village,' I retorted.

I wasn't sure this was true, but I had to contradict him somehow.

'Yes, it would be the perfect complement to the executive homes Mr Bolt is kindly providing,' replied McCreedy.

Providing, indeed. He made it sound as if Bolt was giving them away, rather than turning a hefty profit on one of Little Pride's last green spaces.

'Then why did it stand empty for so long before I bought it?' I blurted, before realising I was arguing against my own cause.

'Precisely because it was not classed as residential,' oozed McCreedy. 'With change of use granted, it would have been snapped up by some local young couple within hours of hitting the market.'

'I rest my case,' added Bolt. 'Although all the better if it was first restored to its former glory by an experienced professional builder familiar with the local vernacular.'

Who would no doubt add extensions, a hot tub and all manner of fancy features to make it match the high spec of his new executive homes, according to Robert Praed, but I did not say that. Staging a public slanging match would not be politic. Instead, I tried to wrap this difficult conversation up with an indisputable conclusion.

'But what you're both forgetting,' I said, trying to keep a triumphant note out of my voice, 'is that Nell Little's Curiosity Shop is no longer for sale, and that it's providing the perfect one-person home for me, while I maintain its retail presence. The best of both worlds, wouldn't you say?'

Bolt stared at me in defiance.

'It may not be for sale right now, but I wager it will be before long. There's no real demand for a tatty old junk shop in a pretty village like this. It just lowers the tone. It's an AONB, see.' He turned to his partner in crime. 'Area of Outstanding Natural Beauty. Now, while you and your good colleagues are here' – he waved his hand at the rest of the party without looking at them – 'why don't you join me for morning coffee at The Quarrymen's Arms?'

There was a murmur of approval from the suited masses.

Two could play at that game.

'Or if you'd prefer to host them on your building site, Mr Bolt, I'd be happy to bring a tray of coffees to you there? With my compliments, of course.'

Bolt glared at me.

'I've already booked four tables at the pub, see,' he snapped. 'We must support our rural public houses, eh, ladies and gentlemen?'

A murmur of assent rippled through the crowd, and they began to file out of the door, turning right towards the village pub. Last to leave was the pink-haired lady, who lingered to speak to me out of earshot of her colleagues.

She produced a card from her jacket pocket – *Felicity Stride, Archaeology Officer* – and raised her eyebrows at me in encouragement.

'Archaeology officer?' I queried. 'Do you usually come out for change-of-use inspections? I wouldn't have expected that to fall under your remit.'

Felicity shook her head. 'No, not normally, but I wangled my way onto this trip as I'm keeping a close eye on what Terence Bolt is up to. The pre-building site survey was approved while I was on holiday last year, and I'm not happy about it. I think it was rushed through in my absence on purpose. I reckon someone's got something to hide. Do let me know if you spot anything untoward, won't you? You can call me in the strictest confidence.'

'Thanks very much, Felicity, I will,' I replied. 'I hope you're right. I admit my hopes rose when one of his labourers brought me a few bits and pieces he'd dug up on the site, but it was nothing remarkable, just the kind of old bottles and broken crocks you might find anywhere in cottage gardens of a certain age. But I'll be sure to let you know if I spot anything of genuine archaeological interest.'

If Bolt could have friends on the council fighting his corner, why shouldn't I? I wasn't doing anything wrong, just being vigilant – and hopeful.

'By the way, if you're ever passing through Little Pride with time to spare, do drop in for a coffee. I'd love to have a chat with you about your role on the council. It sounds like a fascinating job. I used to work at the city museum, and I'll have to feed my interest in history in other ways now. Perhaps we might offer talks together staged here at my shop, or in the village hall? I'm sure we could devise an interesting programme between us.'

Felicity's face brightened. I guessed she'd feel far more at home here than in the newly built modern council offices with a load of pompous men in suits.

'Thanks, Alice, I'd like that very much.'

As I watched her break into a jog to catch up with her colleagues, I was unsure whether I'd won or lost this round with

Bolt and McCreedy. But at least I had found a kindred spirit on the council.

23

PICKING UP THE PIECES

That afternoon, as I sat on my terrace drinking coffee, a wave of panic swept through me. It had been rash of me to offer the council officers refreshments when I'd only just applied to register my café. Even though they'd refused my invitation and gone to the pub, I wouldn't have put it past McCreedy to mobilise the council's health inspectors to review my premises.

Then I realised: food hygiene was nothing to do with the planning department. The subject wouldn't even be on their radar. I could relax a little, even though it had yet to be proven whether or not I was living next door to a killer.

I'd got so used to welcoming strangers to the shop by now that when late afternoon the familiar figure of Robert Praed strolled in, with a small girl aged about six clutching his hand, I did a double take. Robert gave me a cheerful smile, clearly happy in the company of his diminutive companion.

'Hello, Alice, this is Tilly, my granddaughter. Tilly, this is Alice. She runs the shop now.'

'Hello, Tilly.' I leaned across the counter to lower my face to her height. 'Do you live in Little Pride, or are you just visiting?'

'Actually, I live in Great Pride with Mummy and Daddy, but I go to Little Pride Primary School, and Grandpa picks me up sometimes when he's here.'

She dropped Robert's hand to put her arms around his waist in a hug.

Robert ran a hand over her silky, light-brown hair.

'I'm abroad so often on business that when I am in Little Pride, I like to play an active part in Tilly's childhood.' He lowered his voice as Tilly skipped off to look round the shop. 'They grow up too fast, don't they?'

'So everyone says. Not that I have any children of my own to judge by.'

'Ah, I see.' When he looked slightly embarrassed at having exposed my childless state, I was touched by his sensitivity.

'It's OK, though,' I added. 'I'm fine with that.' Although whenever I thought much about it, I really wasn't. 'Still, always good to see other people's children – and to hand them back afterwards, ha ha.'

I gazed at Tilly, thinking how lucky Robert was to be able to collect her after school. Their time together would always be special to them both, long after Tilly was grown up.

Robert deftly changed the subject as if to spare my feelings. 'I like being involved with Tilly's school because I went to Little Pride Primary myself. Not much has changed since then, apart from the technology, of course – whiteboards where there were once blackboards, and report cards printed out rather than handwritten in fountain pen.'

'I suppose it's hard for such a small school to find the budget to make many improvements.'

I guessed from the size of the village that the school roll might not reach three figures.

'Exactly right, Alice. I keep trying to donate money and goods to them, but you wouldn't believe how difficult the council makes it. My last suggested donation of a new classroom block was turned down on the basis that it might threaten the survival of other local village schools, as everyone would want to send their kids here. It seems they'd rather go on teaching in tumbledown rooms in which the children have to wear their coats in winter to keep warm because the old building is so poorly insulated.'

While we were talking, Tilly was having fun trying on the necklaces and bracelets displayed in peach, pressed-glass dishes on an Edwardian dressing table.

'Speaking of the council, I had a surprise visit from the planning department this morning,' I told him. 'They were checking out a new application for change of use from retail to residential.'

'That was quick,' he said. 'Did you apply before you moved in?'

'I didn't, but Bolt did.'

Robert tutted and turned away. 'He doesn't give up, does he? But what about you? Would you like change of use even if they granted it?'

'Now that I'm beginning to settle in, I don't think I would now. If I go about it in the right way, I might make a living from the shop rather than having to get another day job. I have plenty of stock, and I'm computer savvy, so I can sell online too. Plus, I know a lot about domestic social history, which will help me identify products and price them right. The rest of the property is plenty big enough for me to live in, and there's potential for me to turn it into a lovely home.'

Robert nodded his approval.

'Besides,' I added, 'I wouldn't give the loathsome Terence Bolt the satisfaction.'

Robert grinned. 'Atta girl.' Then he turned to Tilly. 'Come on, sweetheart, let's make Alice's day a little more profitable, shall we?

You can choose one thing. Anything you like as a special treat to celebrate the shop's reopening.'

Tilly dropped the green plastic earrings she'd been examining back into a basket of junk jewellery. 'Thanks, Grandpa. I'm going to have a good look at everything now.'

Robert turned back to me with a proud smile. 'She's got her grandfather's business sense. She'll be looking for the best deal she can find. But I don't spoil her, if that's what you're thinking, so I'm afraid this won't be a regular occurrence. Most other days when I pick her up, she'll have to make do with lemonade and a bun.'

As he fondly watched Tilly wander about the shop to choose her treat, I hoped he meant they'd sometimes call for afternoon tea on the terrace.

'I'll make us both a coffee while she's choosing,' I offered. 'On the house.'

I saw it as a loss leader to encourage their future visits. With appalling selfishness, I found myself hoping that there wasn't a Grandma Sponge on the scene to share the experience.

* * *

Just as we were finishing drinking our coffee, the little girl made her decision. She approached the counter with a cardboard box in both hands, its contents clinking as she walked. As she reached up to set it on the counter, I realised it was the batch of tiny stone tiles Barnaby had brought round the day before. I hadn't even taken a proper look at them yet to price them, which was remiss of me.

'I'd like these please, Alice,' said Tilly, with the tone of a child who always knows her own mind. 'If that's all right with you, Grandpa.'

Robert dipped his hand into the box and brought out a few of he small tiles. He arranged them in his palm.

'They could do with a good wash,' he said with uncertainty in his voice. 'Are you sure you wouldn't rather have a pretty necklace, darling?' He caught my eye. 'I can see my daughter having forty fits if I deliver Tilly home with a box of grubby fragments of broken pottery. Belinda's very houseproud, but that's Great Pride for you.'

'Is Great Pride really so different from Little Pride?' I asked. 'I'd just assumed it was the same only bigger.'

Robert grinned. 'Oh no, it's much posher. Little Pride was home to the workers, whereas Great Pride was where most of the gentry and the professionals lived, with the exception of Little Pride's Big House. It's more for aspirational types that seek the Cotswolds out for prestige, like pop stars and politicians. Belinda's not forgiven me yet for buying back my boyhood home in Little Pride when the Old Rectory in Great Pride was on the market at the same time. It hasn't been home to the clergy for decades. The Church of England sold it off long ago, and since then it's been poshed up something chronic by subsequent owners. Who ever heard of a rectory with its own sauna, gym and cinema? It's enough to make you want to take the cloth.'

I laughed, and Tilly tugged at his sleeve.

'I'm sure this is what I want, Grandpa, because we're doing the Romans at school, and I can use them to play at mosaics. Miss Blinken said they loved mosaics in the olden days. We'll be going to see some real live ones near Cirencester for our summer class trip. We'll go on a coach and take packed lunches and everything.'

'That must be Chedworth Roman Villa,' I said. I'd had some dealings with Chedworth when I worked at the Broadwick City Museum. 'There are lots of mosaics at the Corinium Museum in Cirencester too. Well done for making the connection with the ancient Romans, Tilly.'

I peered more closely at the small pieces on Robert's palm.

'You're right, they're very reminiscent of ancient Roman mosaics. Even the colours are spot on – local cream-coloured lime-stone, terracotta and pale-blue lias. The thickness and size and neat edges are just right too. Oh, my.'

I glanced up at Robert. His eyes were wide in astonishment.

'I think you're thinking what I'm thinking,' he said.

Robert turned the pieces over in his hand, scrutinising them more closely. I dipped my hand into the box and brought out a pearlescent fragment.

'And this could be Roman glass,' I said, holding it up to the light.

As happened so often in the museum, my spine tingled at the notion of holding in my hand something touched by human beings hundreds or even thousands of years before.

I wished I'd looked properly at the tiles before the council plan-ners' visit. Then I could have showed them to Felicity for a second opinion. Not that she would have been able to take any action against Bolt's development without proof of where they'd come from. I could only give her Barnaby's word for that, and she'd need to make her own inspection before she could wade in, overturning the existing survey approval.

'Where did you say these came from?' Robert asked slowly. 'Did one of the villagers bring them in on Saturday?'

I shook my head. 'No, Bolt's labourer, Barnaby, traded them with me for coffee and a sandwich.' I widened my eyes at the mention of his name, which I hoped made clear I had no plans to mention Barnaby's murder in front of his granddaughter. 'Earlier, he'd brought a load of old glass bottles in exchange for tea and cake.'

'Does Terence Bolt know about your wheeler-dealing with his workforce?'

'Yes, and he came round to complain about it before *you know what* happened. Well, he knows about the bottles, anyway. He was all for chucking the whole lot in the skip. So, he can't really complain, even if Barnaby did sneak them offsite when Bolt wasn't looking. Bolt just wanted to press on with his build. He seems quite the slavedriver.'

'I gather he's up to his ears in loans,' said Robert. 'He'll be keen to complete this development to pay off his debts as soon as possible if he's to stay in business, so he won't take kindly to shirkers. He was doing OK until Covid came along and put the brakes on everything for him. Still, he should make a handsome profit provided he can sell these houses.'

We fell silent for a moment, no doubt both considering the various possibilities. Had Bolt uncovered an ancient Roman settlement or just a historic dumping ground? If the former, there might be a mosaic floor or even the remains of a whole villa lying until now undetected beneath the paddock. And if Bolt knew about it, would he have the integrity to preserve it, even though it would mean delaying or even cancelling the building project? I could guess the answer.

Robert took a deep breath. 'I don't trust him, Alice. Nor did Barnaby, if he felt the need to sneak these relics out without him seeing.'

'Barnaby seemed like a decent chap, but I don't think he had the historical knowledge to recognise archaeological remains if they fell on his head. He struck me as more of an IKEA man.'

'So, what you're saying is that someone with that knowledge ought to inspect the site pronto before any more damage can be done?' The gleam in his chestnut-brown eyes suggested he wanted in on the adventure. 'Preferably accompanied by someone with a bit of muscle to do any extra excavation as needed.' He raised an arm, Popeye style. 'OK, I might not have the heft of your late builder friend, but I've got enough strength for a spot of light digging. You must come and visit my garden sometime, by the way, and see what's on my side of that great wall.'

I was glad that with all his money, he still took an interest in his garden, although no doubt when he was off on his travels, he'd hire a local to keep it ticking over.

'Or I could ask Danny. You know, my colleague from the museum. The one romantically involved with the triplets.'

Robert's eyes twinkled at my teasing.

'Anyway, time is of the essence, as they're breaking new ground every day,' he went on. 'From the road, it looks like they've already turned over a large part of the plot closest to you, but the part where the donkeys' stable used to be seems as yet untouched.'

He was silent for a moment.

'So, what do you say we pay a little reconnaissance visit this evening?' he continued, turning his big, brown eyes on me. I couldn't resist. 'We can climb over the fence in your back garden so that no one sees us from the street. Bolt need never know.'

'No, and if our suspicions are unfounded, no harm done. Our consciences should be clear. But if we do find something, I know just the person to bring in. Felicity Stride, the council's archaeology officer. She was here this morning with the busload from the planning department. She told me the pre-build survey was completed and signed off while she was on holiday, but she has reason to believe whoever did it is covering something up.'

Tilly, who had been assembling a mosaic picture of a flower on the counter while we'd been talking, tugged at his sleeve. I'd been so engrossed in our plotting that I'd almost forgotten she was there.

'That's lovely, Tilly,' he said, his voice sincere and proud.

'Can you take a picture of it on your phone, please, Grandpa?' she asked.

I smiled.

'Good idea,' I said. 'Then you can show it to your grandma when you go back next door.'

She paused to fit a piece of blue lias into the centre of her flower.

'I haven't got a grandma,' she said placidly.

I bit my lip at my tactlessness.

'I'm sorry,' I began, before Robert came to my rescue.

'Daddy's mummy is called Granny, isn't she, Tilly?' he put in. 'And Daddy's daddy is Grampy.'

'Yes, Grandma died before I was born,' said the little girl. 'That's why I say I haven't got one, but of course I have. It's just that she's up in heaven.' She turned her eyes skywards. 'Sorry, Grandma, that's not your fault. I love you all the same.'

Robert gulped.

'My wife died in a car accident,' he said, his voice catching in his throat. 'It was instant, and she didn't suffer.'

No, but you did, and you still do, I thought, seeing his eyes well up.

I crouched down to put my face on a level with hers.

'My daddy is in heaven too,' I told her, by way of moral support.

She beamed. 'They probably know each other, then. That's nice.' She returned her attention to her flower design. 'So please may I have these mosaic tiles, Grandpa? I can't find anything else Roman in the shop.'

It was hard to refuse her, but I needed to hang on to what might be vital evidence to show Felicity. Then I had a brainwave.

'There are some lovely old linen sheets over there, Tilly.' I pointed to a wooden clothes horse. 'You could make a really authentic toga with proper linen, or if your mum or dad are any good at sewing, you could turn it into a long tunic like Roman ladies used to wear.'

The dressing-up box at the museum was always popular with

children of Tilly's age. Most of the contents were made from cheap, artificial fibres, artfully cut and sewn by volunteers to look convincing to a child's imagination.

I knew the price of the linen sheets reflected their high quality and desirability, but I didn't doubt Robert could afford it. We watched as Tilly selected a snow-white sheet and brought it to the counter.

'Maybe I could also get an old necklace to put in my hair, like Roman ladies did. The ancient Romans were very good at hair-dressing.' She turned pleading eyes on Robert.

So much for her only being allowed one thing, but I wasn't about to point that out.

'You can have a string of beads for free if you buy a linen sheet,' I offered.

The child grinned at my conspiracy and returned to the china bowl of cheap junk jewellery where she picked out a string of imperial purple beads.

Robert smiled at her fondly as he reached for his wallet.

'You've inherited your grandpa's negotiating skills, my darling,' he said. Then he turned to me. 'And you drive an irresistible bargain, Mrs Carroll.'

'It's Miss Carroll, actually, Mr Praed,' I replied with mock primness.

He may have thought I didn't notice him glance at the bare ring finger of my left hand.

'So shall we say eleven o'clock tonight under cover of darkness?'

'It's a date,' I replied, before covering my mouth with my hand. I hadn't meant to put it in those terms. After all, this was merely an investigative venture by neighbours who shared a common interest in preserving local history.

He watched Tilly crown herself with the string of beads. 'If you say so, Miss Carroll.'

Before I could think of a suitable reply, he'd laid two twenty-pound notes on the counter, scooped up the linen sheet and was striding out of the shop holding his granddaughter's hand.

'See you later,' he called over his shoulder as he held the door open for Tilly to skip out into the sunshine.

24

DANNY'S CAUTION

'Let me get this straight. You've got a date after dark with a man you hardly know in a place where no one can see you. Are you sure that's wise?'

Despite being a few years younger than me, Danny had an embarrassing knack of being the grown-up in our relationship. Picturing his reproving expression at the other end of the phone, I was glad I'd opted for a voice-only WhatsApp so I couldn't see it.

'If you're going to put it that way, I've known him for years by reputation. I know I just told you his name's Bob Sponge, but that's only what they call him here in the village. His real name is Robert Praed, the washing-up sponge magnate.'

Danny gave a wry laugh. 'Those aren't words you'd normally string together. But yes, I do know who you mean. My mum swears by his products. She reckons that his sponges are more hygienic than normal washing-up sponges, for some reason. Something to do with the material they are made of being naturally antibacterial, like dingo drool.'

'Ugh! You've put me right off.'

Danny's mum was a pharmacist, and he was always sharing her

horror stories in the staff restroom, such as the healing powers of wild dogs' saliva, as used by Indigenous Australians to heal wounds.

'Doesn't mean he's an OK guy to go off with into a dark building site in the dead of night, though,' said Danny.

'It's hardly the dead of night. We're meeting at eleven o'clock, not the early hours of the morning. Besides, the site is on the main road, right next door to me. If anything happened and I screamed, neighbours would surely hear, and they'd come running. They always seem to know what everyone in the village is doing in any case. To be honest, for all our subterfuge, I'm not really expecting to get away with this visit undetected. The neighbours see everything around here in the daytime at least. Not so much when the street-lights go out.'

I immediately realised we should have made our rendezvous at midnight for exactly this reason.

'That's assuming you'd have the opportunity to scream. What if he crept up behind you?'

'Danny, I'm sure he's perfectly respectable, or else he wouldn't be at the helm of such a successful company.'

The line went quiet for a moment before Danny replied. 'Wasn't there something in the news a few years ago about his wife's death? You don't think—'

'For goodness' sake, that was a car accident. If he was going to murder his wife, which I'm sure he would never have done, he could hardly have engineered a car crash.'

While defending my plan, and Robert's intentions, Danny's questions were making me slightly uneasy. After all, why else would I be telling Danny, unless to ensure that someone knew where to look for me if I went missing? Just because Robert was good with his granddaughter and had spent money in my shop didn't mean he was a safe companion on a dark night in a field.

I tried to put an end to the conversation.

'OK, Danny, if it makes you feel any better, I'll phone you after I get back, so you know I'm safe.'

A note of relief crept into his voice. 'I'll be here. I won't be asleep until about midnight anyway, as I'm planning to binge-watch the rest of the *I, Claudius* box-set after I've eaten.'

'Didn't you have enough of the ancient Romans at work today?' I teased him. 'That's like Nigel Slater sitting down to watch *Master-Chef* on his night off.'

Danny laughed. 'You flatter me, Alice. Anyway, phone me whenever you get back, even in the middle of the night. I shan't sleep until I've heard from you.'

It was my turn to feel better.

'Now get to the interesting bit,' he went on. 'What exactly is it you're expecting to find there? Buried treasure? Dead bodies? Or are you just going to lay a wreath in memory of the donkeys?'

Not wanting to make a fool of myself to a fellow professional if I was wrong, I decided to keep him in suspense. 'I'll tell you when I call you later on.'

Danny huffed. 'OK, be like that. Just don't let Bob Moneybags make you do anything you don't want to.'

'Danny, I'm fifty, not fifteen. I appreciate you being protective of my safety, but I don't need a lecture on morals. Besides, after being exclusive with Stephen for over twenty-five years, I'm hardly about to leap into bed with the first single man who comes along.'

'I didn't mean like that, you twit,' he retorted. 'I mean, as in breaking the law. You do realise that by entering the building site uninvited, you're trespassing? Think how you'd feel if you found that builder guy wandering around your garden in the dead of night.'

'You mean Magnus?' I gulped. 'Or Barnaby's ghost?'

Frankly, I wouldn't have wanted to find either lurking in my vegetable patch.

'I mean the developer. What's his name? Hammer? Spanner?'

'Close. It's Bolt.'

That would be quite a different matter. Small and wiry Bolt may have been, but he had a constant air of threat about him.

'Point taken,' I added. 'Thanks for your support, Danny. I'll let you know how it panned out as soon as I'm back.'

'Anyway, my kitchen timer's just pinged, so I must go,' he said tersely. 'Just be careful.'

25

A DATE AFTER DARK

It might have been over the top to change into all black, but given the vigilance of the neighbours, I thought it better to look as inconspicuous as possible. Without the ambient lights of the city and with few streetlights in Little Pride, the nights were very dark out here. When a neighbour's black cat had prowled across my garden one night, all I could see of it at first were two tiny, reflective, orange discs. They don't call those studs in the middle of the road cats' eyes for nothing.

When Robert knocked on my front door, I opened it to find another all-black silhouette.

'And all because the lady loves Milk Tray,' he quipped.

Was he conceited to liken himself to the bearer of the box of chocolates in the classic television advertisement? To be fair, he was in good shape for his age, with not an ounce of spare flesh as far as I could see. Not that I could see any flesh at all just then beyond his hands and face.

I stepped aside to let him in, and he led the way to the back door with as much assurance as if my cottage was his own. That unnerved me.

'You seem to know your way around,' I remarked.

'Oh, everybody in Little Pride knows their way around your cottage, and my house too. And around everyone else's house that has ever been on the market in this village. As soon as a *For Sale* sign goes up outside a house in the village, or in Great Pride, they're all on the blower to the estate agent arranging visits. They've no intention of buying, of course. They just want a good nose.'

I baulked at the notion of Maudie Frampton and the rest trooping through my cottage as if it was public property, like the museum.

'Don't the estate agents mind? They must have a lot of wasted journeys.'

Robert waved his hands to dismiss my concern. 'Oh no, they love it. It means they can tell their clients they're getting lots of viewings. Although to be fair, the savvier agents organise open days to mop up local demand, rather than having to trek out here every other day. Now, let's go, before the moon disappears behind those clouds. Rain's forecast later tonight, but it should be clear and dry for the next half hour or so – perfect for our mission.'

With that, he led the way into my back garden, leaving the door ajar behind us.

The boundary fence between my property and the old paddock was about waist height. I put my hands on top, ready to climb over, hoping the slats would bear my weight. Then I felt warm hands on my waist.

'Allow me,' said Robert – a command rather than a question – as he lifted me up into the air.

I bent my knees as he swung me over to clear the fence. Then stretched my legs to place my feet gently on the other side, where the ground level was a little higher than in my garden. Next Robert grabbed an old plastic milk crate that was lying on my lawn to serve as a mounting block. He placed it beside the fence and stepped up onto it. Then he simply strode over the fence to land beside me. He rubbed his hands together enthusiastically.

'Right, let's go and see what we can find.' He pulled a slim, aluminium torch from his back pocket and flicked it on. 'That's obviously where they've been excavating most recently.' He pointed to a grass-free rectangle of loose soil a few metres away, one of several spaces marked out with metal pegs and fluorescent-yellow, plastic ribbons, the same shade as *Crime Scene – Do Not Enter* tape. I looked around, half expecting to see SOCO officers in white hazard suits making their way towards us.

'I suppose each ribbon marks a space where a new house will go,' I said. 'This one's going to be awfully close to my cottage. I'm not very happy about that. I didn't mind donkeys putting their furry noses over my fence, but I don't want people peering through my side windows.'

Robert led the way to the spot he'd indicated. I dawdled behind him, a little unnerved by the way he'd hoisted me into the air without my permission. I didn't mind the metaphorical notion of being swept off my feet by a handsome man, but I hadn't realised he was so strong. Remembering Danny's concerns, I decided to keep him in my sights at all times until I was safely back inside my cottage.

'Perhaps we should have brought a spade, or at least a hand trowel,' he observed as he kneeled by the deep trench within the marked space. 'But hang on, the soil seems loose enough for us to scrabble through it by hand. Would you like to hold the torch while I do my impression of a puppy-dog digging up a bone?'

He passed me his torch, its metal casing still warm from his touch. I trained the beam on the trench as Robert kneeled down and leaned forward, scooping up loose earth with both hands. After a minute or two, he reached compacted soil at the bottom of the trench and began to sift handfuls of the crumbly, dark top layer through his fingers.

'It's luscious soil,' he remarked. 'Rich and dark and full of nutrients after decades of being used as an animal paddock.'

'Enriched by all that donkey manure, I suppose.' I grimaced, glad it wasn't me that was grubbing about in it with bare hands.

'Here, shine your torch on this bit,' he said, sitting back and pointing.

When I obeyed, the peaty blackness turned out to be peppered with tiny, coloured pottery fragments exactly matching what Barnaby had given me, and which Tilly had coveted for her Roman project.

'Terracotta, limestone and blue lias,' I murmured, my heartrate quickening. 'But no sign of cement. Tile cement, not Bolt's building modern stuff – the mortar ancient Roman craftsmen used to fix their mosaics into place. They're all just loose. This could have been a dump of spare pieces left over from a big project nearby. I'm surprised the mosaic artists didn't take them away once they'd finished. Another explanation might be that this was once the site of a mosaic maker's workshop rather than completed floors.'

'Will a stash of loose Roman tiles be enough to halt the build?' asked Robert.

I wrinkled my nose. 'I doubt it. I think it would just be treated as an interesting archaeological find. The powers that be might just lift the horde of tesserae – that's the technical term for Roman mosaic tiles – and whisk them off to a museum or university, then allow the build to proceed. Felicity Stride will tell us for sure. We have to report this to her, and not only because we want to stop Bolt's development. If we didn't, we'd be complicit in concealing ancient artefacts, which is against the law.'

I turned to look at him. 'Even so, wouldn't it be lovely if we were able to stop the build and return this site to the peaceful paddock it was before? I hate to think what happened to those lovely donkeys.' Tears sprang to my eyes. 'You don't suppose Bolt had them slaughtered and turned into cat food or glue, do you?'

Embarrassed by my sudden rush of emotion, I wandered over to the former site of the donkeys' stable, where the ground was as yet unbroken. The outline of its foundations was still visible in the long grass. The moon shining brightly in the clear, starry sky, turned the neat rectangle almost luminescent. The outline on the ground was so clear that I didn't need the torch to find it. I heard Robert's footsteps behind me on hard soil. It must have been tamped down hard by the machinery thundering about the site all week.

I gulped. 'At least the donkeys wouldn't have known what Bolt's plans were.'

I jumped slightly as Robert laid a warm hand on my shoulder. I hoped he just meant to comfort me.

'You big softie,' he said gently. 'When Bolt bought the paddock, he didn't acquire the donkeys as sitting tenants, any more than you took on Nell Little when you purchased her Curiosity Shop. Actually, I bought the donkeys from the paddock's previous owner before Bolt acquired it and rehomed them on one of my farms near Moreton-in-Marsh.'

'Really? I didn't know you were a farmer too.'

In the moonlight, I noticed his shy smile. 'Not exactly, but I buy failing farms and inject a bit of cash to revive them, employing the farmers that used to work the land. It's all part of my financial strategy. You know what they say: you can't go wrong investing in land because they're not making any more of it.'

I bent down to run my hand along the rough, rocky line. It reminded me of a drystone wall that had been razed to ground level.

'Well, it doesn't look as if anything will grow here for a long time. It's surprisingly barren for a field of such fertile earth.'

Robert shrugged. 'Perhaps we'll never know why. Anyway, at least we've got what we came for: clear evidence of Roman mosaic tiles on the site. You'd better take a few photos so we're not asking Felicity Stride and the council just to take your word for it. Old Bolt's got far too many chums on the council who would give him the benefit of any doubt, so you will have to provide irrefutable evidence.'

I straightened my back, my eyes still on the bare patch of earth. '*I* will? *My* word? I thought we were in this together.'

Suddenly, I felt vulnerable. Without Robert's backing, would the council believe me, a newcomer and an outsider, over their mate Bolt?

Robert cleared his throat. 'I'm afraid the council always seems to look for reasons to thwart anything I suggest, even when I'm literally giving them something of value, like my proposed donation to the village school. So, I think it would be better if you approach them in the first instance. I'll back you up at the right time and behind the scenes. I don't want this housing development any more than you do. What Little Pride doesn't need is fancy houses for' – he paused – 'more rich, old, white, straight blokes like me.'

I laughed. 'Actually, Robert, I think more people like you preserving historic houses and looking out for their neighbours are exactly what Little Pride needs.'

He smiled again, his teeth bright in the moonlight. 'OK, but maybe I don't want the competition.'

When he reached for my hand, I thought he was after his torch, but the hand he took was not the one with the torch in it.

'Come on then,' he said. 'Let's take a few photos before we lose the moonlight.'

'Won't we just be framing ourselves as trespassers, though?'

I wanted to keep on the right side of the law, but Robert shook his head.

'I don't think showing the tiles your workman friend brought in will be sufficient proof to stop the build. He could have got them from anywhere. Besides, you don't need to show Bolt the photos – just send them to Felicity Stride, and she can take over.'

I let him lead me by the hand to our earlier excavation, then he trained the torch on some of the tesserae while I took pictures on my phone.

'I'll take a few on mine too as backup,' he said, when I'd finished.

'I'll email my images to Felicity before I go to bed,' I said.

After taking a dozen shots from various angles, I was just about to slip my phone back into my pocket when it began to vibrate. Knowing we were going to be trespassing, I'd had the foresight to turn the ringer off before we'd set out.

My heart began to pound at the thought the police might be onto us. I was already in enough trouble with the law about my driving licence. Then the familiar profile photo of the caller made me breathe a sigh of relief. 'Oh, Danny, thank goodness it's you,' I whispered.

I noticed Robert glance at me, then look away.

'Just thought I'd take the opportunity between episodes to see how you were getting on.'

'I'm fine,' I replied. 'It's OK, don't worry.' I turned my back to Robert, hoping to muffle what Danny was saying, just in case he made any remarks that I wouldn't want Robert to overhear. 'But I can't talk now. I'll call you when I'm back indoors, OK?'

'OK,' he replied. 'Make sure you do.'

'Bye,' I said hastily, before pressing the red button to end the call.

Robert slipped his phone into the back pocket of his jeans. 'OK, let's head home before Neighbourhood Watch dobs us in.'

Not sure whether I was disappointed or relieved that he didn't lift me over the fence this time, I offered Robert a coffee or something stronger as we entered my cottage, but he declined politely and headed for the front door.

26

TAPPING DANNY

I'd just settled down with a comforting hot chocolate on my own when my phone vibrated again.

'I hope I'm not interrupting anything,' said Danny.

I sighed. I was starting to feel henpecked. 'Danny, I said I'd phone you back, and I was just about to. It was lucky my phone was on vibrate just now or my ABBA ringtone would have announced our presence to anyone within earshot. Anyway, I'm back at home now, and before you ask, yes, I'm on my own. Mission accomplished.'

'My, my,' he said. I could tell he was smirking. 'So is your friend Bolt finally facing his Waterloo as a result of your surreptitious visit?'

'He certainly is. Looks like a stash of tesserae were left there by Brito-Roman mosaic workmen. I'm convinced the paddock was the site of some kind of workshop for cutting tiles. I'm going to email Felicity Stride, the council's archaeology officer, before I go to bed, to alert her to our find. As belt-and-braces, I'll phone her first thing in the morning too. I don't suppose finding a cache of random tesserae will be enough to stop the build altogether, but even if it just slows it down, it will teach Bolt not to be so arrogant.'

'So, were the tesserae very widespread or just in a single cache?'

'We only really investigated one trench, which had already been dug by Bolt's team. They haven't broken ground on the whole site yet, so I'm hoping the council will want to check over the paddock before he goes any further. And you never know, it might lead to a more significant find that will scupper his development forever.'

'It's quite a big field, as I recall,' said Danny. 'It could possibly be big enough to house a small villa. Perhaps the outline we saw on Google Earth is the remains of its walls.'

'Isn't that how farmers have often discovered Roman remains in their fields, by noticing an outline free of crops? Then when they've excavated, they found whole villas, complete with mosaic floors.'

'Well, the remains of villas, anyway. Remember, after the Romans had withdrawn from Britain, local settlers often cannibalised the materials from the old Roman settlements to build their own houses. But yes, that's happened a lot in the Cotswolds and elsewhere. Blimey, Alice, this could be a really significant find. I wish I'd been there with you tonight to see it for myself.'

I felt bad now for not inviting him. Perhaps I'd had a subconscious motive for spending time alone with Robert. If so, it was wrong of me to prioritise Robert when Danny had been such a good friend to me, especially when he knew so much about the ancient Romans. I tried to redeem myself.

'I'll tip you the wink as soon as the archaeological officer comes to see it, I promise. And I'll make it clear that you were the one that realised the potential of the site. That should score you some brownie points with the awful Glen. And if you get your picture in the paper pointing out the find, you'll probably get some publicity for the museum as a bonus.'

'I might even be asked to go on telly.' He sounded pleased. 'This could be the sort of find that will make national news.'

'Or attract a documentary team,' I enthused, secretly thinking, *I just want my donkeys back. Or rather, Robert's donkeys. Perhaps one day they might become my step-donkeys.* 'By the way, I've discovered they're still alive,' I added, trying to stop thinking about Robert.

'The ancient Romans? Alice, have you been drinking? I thought you were on the wagon after that incident with your car. Which still isn't ready for collection, by the way.'

'Not the ancient Romans, silly. The donkeys. Robert rehomed them on one of his farms. Isn't that great?'

'Of course he did,' Danny said tersely. 'Anyway, you'd better get your email off to that archaeology officer now, so she sees it first thing in the morning. We don't want old Hammer Man to start dredging up any actual villa before we've had a proper chance to save it.'

'Right away, boss,' I replied. 'And I'll bcc you in on my email for information. But don't say anything to Glen yet. We don't want him stealing our glory like he's done before.'

'I promise,' said Danny.

As soon as we'd ended the call, I went straight to my laptop, glad that I'd hung on to Felicity Stride's business card. There wasn't a moment to lose.

27

IN THE PINK

A soon as I was up and dressed the next day, I called Felicity's direct line, and she picked up straight away. When I introduced myself, I was gratified that she remembered who I was and where we'd met. She hadn't yet seen my message.

'My email is about the building site next door to me, rather than anything to do with my property,' I explained as she fired up her computer. 'I have reason to believe that the old paddock is a site of historical significance, given what the developer's excavations have uncovered on the site so far. But I think Bolt is trying to conceal them so as not to disrupt or delay his build.'

'Historical, you say?' said Felicity, a note of caution in her voice. She probably had lots of false alarms about bits of broken willow pattern and the like. 'Just how historical do you mean? Victorian? Georgian?'

My pulse was racing at what I was about to reveal. 'Roman, ancient Roman. Fourth century Common Era at the latest.'

'Well, it would be,' she replied, 'given that the Romans had all but departed these shores by that point. So what evidence are you basing your claim on?'

I paused for effect, aware of the excitement my announcement would generate in a fellow historian.

'Tesserae.' Such a lovely word. 'A significant stash of Brito-Roman tesserae, in a mix of vernacular materials – terracotta and limestone, and I think blue lias. A darker, harder stone, in any case.'

I heard her gasp. 'How many pieces? Are they just loose, or has Bolt disturbed a mosaic floor? Even if it's just a mosaic-maker's stash, rather than a finished pavement, it would still be potentially a protected find, at least until we've had the chance to remove the pieces.'

'We've only found a pile of random tiles at the moment, but in the far corner of the plot is the kind of bare, rectangular outline in the soil that suggests the subterranean remains of a Roman villa, according to one of my museum colleagues. A small one, but it has to be worth checking out before Terence Bolt can rip it up with his digger. Not all Roman villas were huge estates, were they?'

'Absolutely,' said Felicity. 'There were more modest ones called strip houses, as opposed to those built around one or more court-yards. Those often had good mosaic floors too. And between you and me, I think you're right not to trust Bolt. I could tell when we visited the other day that he wasn't, shall we say, as culturally aware or sensitive as we'd like developers to be. Hey, I've just opened my emails, and I'm looking at your photos. Those tiles look pretty ancient to me. Listen, I'm meant to be going into an internal meeting at ten. Give me five minutes to excuse myself from that, and I'll head straight over to you. I presume Bolt's already at work on the site this morning?'

'Yes, the noise of his machinery woke me up again this morning, although it wasn't as raucous as usual.' I held the phone away from my ear for a moment to capture distant rumbling sounds.

'Do you think you can create a distraction to make him down tools till I get there?'

I hesitated, trying to think of how I might do that.

'Actually, Alice,' Felicity continued, without waiting for me to reply, 'as one historian to another, the only acceptable answer to that question is "yes".'

Felicity's steely determination impressed me. On her previous visit to the site, I'd had the impression she was a little intimidated by her colleagues, but the current circumstances were bringing out her fighting spirit.

'OK, I'll come up with something to delay his progress,' I assured her. 'If I'm not next door in the old paddock when you get here, I'll be in my shop, so just come and find me when you need me.'

'Thanks, Alice, I appreciate your help. See you shortly.'

Without further ado, she ended the call, leaving me with a mental picture of her sprinting to her boss's office to absent herself, then leaping into her car with the speed and enthusiasm of Batman in his Batmobile.

I darted through the dining room to the shop and out of the front door, pausing to lock it behind me. I'd only finalised the insurance for my new business the night before, and I didn't want to invalidate it on the very first day of the policy by leaving the shop unmanned and unlocked.

I marched along the pavement to the entrance of the building site and through the rickety five-bar gate, then stopped to survey the scene for signs of life. There was no one to be seen, until a digger's engine suddenly fired up and I realised the mighty machine was trundling towards me. To my surprise, it wasn't Magnus in the driving seat, but Terence Bolt, a steely scowl on his face, his hands tight on the wheel and ear defenders clamped onto his skull. Surely in Barnaby's absence, it was Magnus's job to drive the digger, not Bolt's. So where was Magnus?

But there was no time to pursue that line of thought now.

'Stop!' I yelled at the top of my voice. Unsure he could hear me, I took the precaution of darting back through the gate and closing it behind me. Surely Bolt wouldn't bulldoze the boundary wall to frighten me – or even to flatten me?

When I waved my arms above my head like a drowning woman signalling for help, to my relief he shut off the engine and slipped the ear defenders down around his neck.

'What?' he shouted, scowling.

'I need to talk to you urgently,' I shouted back, assuming his hearing was reduced at least temporarily from driving such a noisy vehicle. 'I need to ask you an important question.'

Unsure yet what that question might be, I wondered how to play for time. Pretend to faint from fear that he was about to run me over? No, I wasn't going to let him take me for a feeble female. No way would I allow him to feel he had the upper hand over me, even if he did have a great big digger on his side.

Glancing down the high street, I was greatly relieved to espy Andrew Gloster strolling towards us. Thank goodness! He'd be on my side for sure.

'Oh look, here comes Andrew,' I said quickly. I trusted he'd be savvy enough to weed out the nonsense from my despatches before publishing. Bolt, if he knew what was good for him, would want to keep in Andrew's good books, as he'd be wanting him to make only positive reports on the new development.

'Morning, all,' said Andrew jovially. 'How's tricks?'

In a flash, I decided to take Andrew into my confidence. He was a sophisticated type; he'd surely understand the significance of our find the previous night.

'Andrew, I'm so glad you're here,' I said, not looking at Bolt. Look, here's a scoop for you. I've reason to believe that Mr Bolt's uncovered evidence of Roman remains while excavating the paddock, so he'll need to stop work until the council's archaeology officer has been to check them out. She's on her way now.'

Bolt snorted.

'How would you know a thing like that? Have you been trespassing?' He turned to Andrew. 'There's a story for you, Andy. You'd better run a warning in your mag. Get Neighbourhood Watch to keep an eye on her if she's in the habit of snooping about in places where she don't belong.' Then he glared at me. 'Now I'll thank you to get off my land and let me go about my legitimate business. These houses won't build themselves, you know. The sooner my houses here are done, the better for Little Pride. Isn't that right, Andrew? So, for the last time, Alice Carroll, get off my land.'

'I'm not on your land,' I said sweetly. 'I'm on the public highway. But even from here, I can see what looks like Roman tesserae glinting in the sunlight.'

I pointed at the trench to the right of where Bolt had parked the digger.

'Tessa Whatty?' asked Andrew mildly. 'What are they when they're at home?'

He'd clearly decided not to take sides yet. I admired his diplomacy, although disappointed that he hadn't immediately sided with me.

'Tesserae are the small pieces of stone and pottery and occasionally glass that the ancient Romans used to make their mosaics,' I explained.

Bolt rolled his eyes at Andrew. 'She's got a vivid imagination, see. Just a few bits of tatty old domestic china, these are, slung in the garden with the scraps by some old biddy last century. You'll find them in every cottage garden in the village, and probably in yours up at the Big House, Andrew. If you think they're valuable antiques, Alice Carroll, you're off your crust. Doesn't say much for the worthless rubbish in your shop.'

Andrew laid a reassuring hand on my shoulder. 'I admire your vigilance, Alice, but we've all been here a lot longer than you have.' He spoke to me as if I were a child, which made my hackles rise. 'I think we'd all have known if there were valuable antiques lying buried here.'

I'd expected more support from him. Still, at least our row was buying more time for Felicity to arrive.

When Bolt gave a smug grin, his yellow teeth looked as if they'd just been unearthed from the paddock.

'Not necessarily,' I replied. 'Farmers often uncover Roman antiquities in fields that have lain fallow for a long time. Why, not long ago, in Tetbury, they dug up two clay pots of Roman coins undetected for nearly two millennia. Why should Little Pride be exempt from such finds?'

Bolt's manner changed in an instant. 'Roman gold coins, you say? They must have been worth a few bob to whoever found them. Much more than tatty old bits of broken pottery.'

He took a few steps towards the trench and leaned down for closer inspection. I'd found his weak spot: avarice. I decided not to let on about the laws of Crown property versus treasure trove. The hope of enriching himself with what lay beneath the soil might be enough to delay the build while he dug, Long John Silver style, for buried treasure.

'Yes, they were thought to have been buried as some kind of funerary offering,' I continued. 'I believe they were valued at over a quarter of a million pounds.'

Bolt's beady eyes bulged.

'I'll keep an eye open for any more pots of gold,' he began, 'but I gotta keep going, see. I'm on a tight enough schedule as it is.'

Just then Felicity's car pulled up beside us, and she stepped out onto the pavement carrying a green webbing satchel.

'Good morning, Mr Bolt, Mr Praed,' she said, nodding to the men. 'Hello, Ms Carroll.'

Andrew beamed at her as if welcoming an old friend. 'Why, Felicity, how lovely to see you. To what do we owe the pleasure?'

I suppose he needed to keep in with the local council offices to help him research the stories for his magazine.

'It's Mr Bolt I've come to see,' she replied, turning away from Andrew, apparently immune to his charm. 'Mr Bolt, I understand you have found evidence of Roman antiquities on your property, and I'm here to assess their significance before you can make any further advances with your construction.'

Bolt pursed his lips. 'Just a few little bits and pieces of old pottery. Nothing to see here. No need to hold up the work, surely. If we find any buried treasure, we'll let you know.'

I suspected Bolt would only recognise genuine antiquities if he found them in a big wooden chest bearing a skull and crossbones.

'I'll be judge of that, thank you,' Felicity said calmly. 'Now, if you'll kindly allow me site access, we can get on with my preliminary inspection without delay.' She flashed a winning smile as she opened the five-bar gate and entered the paddock. 'I know you want to get on.'

I was about to follow her when Andrew laid his hand on my arm.

'Actually, Alice, it was you I'd come to see, not Bolt. I've had a power cut at the Big House this morning, so I've not had any breakfast yet. I was hoping your shop would be open so I could buy a coffee and some toast.'

I glanced reluctantly after Felicity, who was bending over the trench, picking out tesserae. I wouldn't have put it past Bolt to bash her on the head with a spanner and bury her in the hole in the ground while we weren't looking. Then I chided myself for being over-dramatic. He'd hardly assault and inter her in full view of Andrew Gloster drinking coffee on my tea terrace.

Andrew was looking pointedly at his watch. 'You did say ten o'clock was your opening time in the *Little Pride Parish News*, didn't you?'

He had me there. I could hardly refuse. Before I came to Little Pride, I'd never have believed a little parochial publication could be so influential.

'Well, if it's in the *Parish News*, it must be true,' I replied sweetly. 'If you'd care to come with me back to the Curiosity Shop and take a seat, I'll rustle up a belated breakfast for you right away. But it'll have to be on the house. My café business isn't yet registered to trade.'

'Then you must let me buy you a drink in the pub one night to return the favour,' he said pleasantly, which seemed fair enough.

* * *

Just as Andrew was finishing his toast, I saw Felicity coming up the path, turning over some tesserae in her hand. Andrew got up when he saw her coming and brought his empty cup indoors to the shop counter.

'I'll leave you to chat with your archaeologist chum,' he said mildly. 'I'd be out of my depth.'

'I've got more of those,' I told her as she entered the shop.

'Ooh, really? Can I see them?' She set her satchel on the counter as I fished the box out of the cupboard where I'd stowed it for safe-keeping.

She rifled through the tiles before looking up, her eyes gleaming.

'It never gets old, you know, the feeling of handling something last touched by someone in antiquity.'

'Apart from Barnaby, Robert Praed, his granddaughter Tilly, and me,' I corrected her with a smile. 'But I know what you mean. So, do you think they are genuine?'

She ran her fingertip around the edge of a small cube of terracotta, one side flat and square-edged, the others uneven.

'Yes, absolutely. Look, these pieces haven't been machine-cut, like modern mosaic tiles, nor are they the result of casual breakage. They've been hand-knapped by ancient craftsmen. Carbon-dating will confirm my judgement, or else optically stimulated luminescence.'

'Ooh, I've seen them do that on *Digging for Britain*,' I exclaimed. 'How exciting.'

'But that's not all.' She leaned closer to me and lowered her voice. 'You know that outline you told me about in the far corner?'

I nodded, my eyes widening.

'There's evidence that the top level of soil has been lifted recently and replaced. I sneaked a peek underneath while Bolt was distracted by a phone call, and I'm sure I saw a patch of rather fine example of guilloche. That's a typical pattern used to edge larger Brito-Roman mosaic floors.'

'You mean you think there really is a mosaic floor beneath the paddock?'

She nodded, grinning in excitement. 'And what's more, when you prod the ground enclosed by the rectangle, where the turf is still intact, there's rock-hard resistance consistent with a substantial expanse of complete mosaic floor.'

My mouth fell open. 'But how come no one knew about it before?'

She shrugged. 'It's not unusual in uncultivated land. There's been about sixty such finds in the Cotswolds over the years. Some floors were lifted and removed to museums, others left in situ and reburied to preserve them better. Others have simply never been discovered before.'

'So, I'm not being outlandish in suspecting one might be under Bolt's paddock?'

'Not at all,' said Felicity. 'There must be loads that we've just not come across yet. Still, I can't believe Bolt didn't know this one was there, and if he did, it seems he wasn't going to let on. He was probably planning to bury it under a patio or something, or even pass it off as a modern one, and hope no one cottoned on. Honestly, it makes me mad how greedy some developers can be. Don't they understand that ancient remains like this are finite and irreplaceable? Unlike their dreadful new-builds, which likely won't see this century out.'

I was starting to understand how frustrating Felicity's job could be, out in the real world, as opposed to our work in the Broadwick City Museum.

'So, what are you going to do about it?' I asked. 'Is this enough to stop the build? Please say it'll mean the plot has to revert to being a paddock.'

'That's not up to me. But I doubt he'd be allowed to build on top of it. It's one thing to cover up a mosaic to preserve it, but quite another to stick a damn great modern house over the top. That's definitely not allowed.'

I hugged myself in my excitement.

'I can clap a holding order on him for now,' she went on. 'Ideally, we should have been informed about this before the planning application was granted, if the land had been properly surveyed, which I'd always thought was doubtful. Then they'd have been able to adapt the plans to preserve the mosaic. Preserving in situ is always our preference. Anyway, lots to think about here. First, I'd like to write my notes up and upload my photos before I head back to the office so that I can issue the necessary paperwork to halt work as soon as possible.'

'You can send it to my printer if you like, if it means you can present him with a physical copy of the paperwork before you go,' I offered.

Felicity nodded. 'Brilliant, thanks, Alice, that's perfect. Now, is it OK if I work at one of your café tables? It's a glorious morning.'

She turned her face to the sun and closed her eyes in appreciation.

'Sure. Can I get you a coffee on the house? If your excavations stop the development, I'll give you free coffee for life.'

I wasn't joking.

'Then you'll get off lightly as I don't drink coffee,' she replied with a smile. 'But I'd love a cold drink, if you're offering.'

'Right away,' I said. 'Make yourself comfortable and stay as long as you like. Email me the document when it's done, and I'll send it to my printer.'

As I headed for the kitchen to rustle up a fruit cordial for her, it occurred to me that a smartly dressed businesswoman tapping away at her laptop on my tea terrace would be a good advertisement to anyone else who liked working in cafés. I was getting more optimistic about the prospects of my business by the day.

28

SOMETHING IN THE WATER

Still engrossed in her report an hour later, listening to music through earbuds to block out the building noises from the paddock, Felicity kindly offered to look after the shop for me while I nipped up to the village shop for some milk and tea bags. When I took her a second drink by way of thanks, she told me not to rush. I wondered whether she was sitting tight to keep an eye on Bolt so he didn't fire up his digger to destroy the big mosaic before she could file her report. Cleverly, she was sitting with her back to the paddock so he would not feel he was being watched, but surely she'd hear his digger firing up, even over the sound of her music.

I took the opportunity to make a slight detour to update Coralie on the exciting news. Knowing how she felt about Bolt, I was confident she'd be as pleased as I was at the news that his current project was about to be stopped, at least temporarily. When I told her, she threw her arms around me in a jubilant hug, and we danced an impromptu jig together about her flag-stoned floor of her salon. She made me tell me the whole story of my night-time excursion with Robert – I'd long stopped worrying about being accused of trespass – relishing every detail.

When finally she allowed me to leave, I strolled back down the high street, feeling the most optimistic I'd been since I'd moved to Little Pride. My shop was starting to seem like a viable business, and at least for a while, the dust and noise from Bolt's excavations wouldn't disturb my new rural idyll. The sun warmed my face as I sauntered along, and I brushed my hand against the cottage garden plants that spilled over the drystone walls onto the pavement, releasing a multitude of floral and herbal fragrances.

As I approached my shop, I was surprised to see a cluster of so many people on my tea terrace that they were spilling over onto the pavement. I wondered where so many customers had sprung from in my absence. Perhaps a coachload of tourists had arrived while I was in Suki's Stores or Coralie's Curls. Whatever their source, despite Felicity's offer to hold the fort, I could hardly expect her to cope with such a huge influx of trade while she was officially here on council business. I didn't want to compromise her, nor did I want to miss out on this sudden flurry of potential customers, so I quickened my step.

As I drew closer, I realised the throng of people weren't interested in the shop at all. Instead, they were gathered around Felicity's table. What was she doing, show and tell? Well, that would be OK. The more people who knew about the mosaic, the less likely Bolt would be able to hide it.

'Stand back, nothing to see here,' a man's voice was shouting. Andrew's voice. That was unexpected. He'd left the shop as Felicity had arrived. Perhaps he'd come back for lunch, still plagued by his power cut.

As the onlookers obeyed him and stepped back, talking among themselves, I saw a figure slumped over the café table: Felicity. One arm was hanging loosely by her side; the other was draped across the tabletop, her right hand clutching the antique blue bottle I had used as a vase, one of those that Barnaby had bartered for a cup of coffee. The bottle was hexagonal, and each side was ridged, apart from one flat surface, which bore a single word in raised letters moulded into the glass: *POISON*.

I rushed forward to kneel at Felicity's side, looking up into her face. Her eyes were closed, her mouth open, and her tongue protruding. A pool of dribble had formed at the side of her mouth, but to my relief, she was still breathing, albeit shallowly. Then Bolt emerged from the crowd.

'See? You've poisoned another one!'

When he grabbed the bottle and held it aloft in triumph, I snatched it off him angrily, before realising that both of us had now contaminated the evidence with our fingerprints. I slammed it back on the table, out of Felicity's reach.

'Oh, for goodness' sake, don't be ridiculous. If I was going to poison someone, I'd be a bit more subtle about it.'

I blushed in embarrassment at my crass first reaction.

'I mean, of course I haven't poisoned her. That old bottle was just being used as a vase. It's a complete red herring. Besides, nobody with half a brain would fail to notice that someone has throttled her.'

I nodded at the reddish mark circling her neck beneath the scarf, not daring to touch it for fear of leaving incriminating fingerprints.

'What do you know?' retorted Bolt. 'That could be a cover-up job to hide the real cause. I seen you dosing her up with those weird herbal drinks of yours this morning. You had ample opportunity to slip something dodgy in there, just like you did in Barnaby's coffee.'

The assembled onlookers gave a startled gasp.

'Thank goodness Mr Gloster happened to be passing by when no one else was about and noticed her distress!' said a woman in the crowd.

Bolt's accusation was utter nonsense, but this was no time for squabbling.

'Has someone called an ambulance?' I asked, my mobile at the ready.

Andrew waved his phone. 'It's on its way, Alice. Meanwhile, can I suggest the rest of you disperse to make way for the paramedics?'

Felicity's eyelids fluttered, and I laid my hand gently over hers.

'It's OK, Felicity, you're going to be OK,' I said softly. 'Hang in there.'

I kept talking to her, saying anything that came into my head, to try to keep her conscious until the ambulance arrived. Everyone else but Andrew gradually dispersed from the scene. Even Bolt stopped casting aspersions and sidled back to the paddock, where I could now hear the steady thud of spade in soil, delving further into the trench where we'd seen the loose tesserae. Perhaps he was hoping to find a Little Pride hoard of Roman gold there too.

'I don't remember anything,' croaked Felicity as soon as she could speak. 'Just suddenly everything went dark.'

Then a police car and an ambulance arrived. The policemen immediately began sealing off my terrace with black and yellow *Crime Scene – Do Not Cross* tape, and bagging up anything that took their fancy as evidence, including the bottle and the yellow, pink and green tie-dyed scarf that lay pooled on the table. I didn't remember her wearing it earlier. It would have stood out against her grey trouser suit. Perhaps it had been wielded by her attacker hoping to pass it off as Felicity's own, and the only reason Felicity was holding the bottle was that she'd used it as a weapon to strike her assailant. I hoped the police might find fingerprints or even DNA evidence of a fourth person on the bottle, besides Felicity, Bob and me.

Meanwhile the paramedics checked Felicity's vital signs, one taking notes on an electronic tablet while the other administered various instruments.

'Don't worry, love,' said the one who was clipping an oximeter onto her finger. 'Most important thing is to get you to hospital now and get you checked over. The police can talk to you later. Rest your voice for now and we'll be on our way.' He turned to me. 'I take it you're her friend or partner? Would you like to come with us? You can hop in the ambulance or follow by car if you prefer. That way you can bring her home again easily.'

I exchanged glances with Felicity, and she gave me a slight nod. I guessed she could do with some moral support and a friendly face. Whatever had happened, whoever had attacked her, it must have been a terrifying experience.

'I'll have to hitch a ride with you, I'm afraid,' I replied. 'I don't have my car here at present. It's at a garage in town, getting fixed. They're waiting for a part.'

Felicity pointed to her satchel, into which I'd just packed her tablet, notebook and pen that she'd been using at the table.

'Take my keys,' she croaked. 'It's a council pool car, and the insurance covers any driver. It's a navy-blue Ford Focus, and I've parked it just up the road. The registration is on the key ring.'

I accepted the keys gladly, trying not to think of the disastrous last time I'd driven. It had really shaken my confidence. I still couldn't understand what had come over me that night, even now I'd had plenty of time to consider it in a more detached way. If I hadn't been among friends that night – well, apart from Glen, anyway – I'd have wondered whether my drink had been spiked. Still, now was not to the time to think about that. I needed to put Felicity first. After all, if it wasn't for me, she wouldn't have been here, which – unless she had a stalker – meant she wouldn't have been attacked.

Just then, someone coughed behind me, the forced cough of

someone craving attention. I turned round to find a tall, broad-shouldered policeman towering over me. For a moment, I thought he was about to arrest me.

'Before you go, madam, can I suggest you pack some overnight things for yourself?'

'For me? Don't you mean for Felicity, in case they keep her in overnight?'

'I'm sorry, madam, I do mean for you. You see, we're going to have to ask you to vacate your premises for at least twenty-four hours to allow us to conduct a thorough search following this morning's unfortunate incident. My colleague here will take a statement from you as soon as you return from the hospital and also your prints for exclusion purposes. In the meantime, please leave your mobile phone number, and do not make any travel plans.'

My mouth fell open. Surely they didn't suspect me of attacking Felicity? I gulped. Did they think I might try to flee the country? Perhaps they'd already wired my description to all ports to ensure I didn't escape justice – or whatever technology they used these days.

My heart pounding, I duly gave him my phone number and Danny's address, planning to cadge a bed from him and Martin for the night, even though it would be awkward to see Martin in my newly redundant state. Then I handed over the spare set of keys for the shop and headed to Felicity's car to follow the ambulance.

29

ON THE COUCH

'They requisitioned the poison bottle and Felicity's scarf for fingerprinting,' I told Danny as he pressed a large glass of chilled, dry white wine into my hands. 'If indeed it was Felicity's scarf. I'm thinking her attacker may have brought it with them as their weapon. The police took my fingerprints, again, and yet another statement. This is starting to become a habit.'

I laughed uneasily as I tried to play down my concerns, staring into my glass, as if seeking an escape route through drink. But Danny knew me too well to fall for my charade.

'Honestly, Danny, they made me feel as if I was lying, even though I was telling the truth.'

Danny settled down beside me on Martin's squashy, purple, velvet sofa, a tumbler of sparkling water in his hand.

'Don't worry, that'll just be routine to eliminate you from their enquiries.'

He slipped a comforting arm around me, and I leaned my head on his shoulder.

'But what if the bottle still has traces of poison, and they find the same poison in her system? I put the bottle on the table, even though I didn't intend her to drink out of it. It might still kill her yet – some poisons are very slow-acting and have no antidote, like overdoses of paracetamol. It'll be my responsibility. Surely that would count as manslaughter at the very least? That would spell the end of my café, my shop, and my freedom.' I covered my face with my hands. 'My goodness, Steven's only been gone five minutes, and I'm about to be sent to prison. So much for my new lease of life.'

Danny patted my knee. 'Don't be so daft, Alice. It's not as if you served her drink in the poison bottle. You know you've done nothing wrong. The real culprit is the person who tried to strangle her. Have a little faith in our criminal justice system. They'll find her real attacker in no time. He or she is bound to have been caught on camera somewhere.'

I shook my head. 'Not in Little Pride, they won't, for the simple reason that we don't have any surveillance cameras out there, other than on a few people's front doorbells. There are certainly none trained on my house.'

'What about next door? If you're so matey with that Sponge guy, he'll surely share any evidence he's captured. I bet a big shot like him will have loads of security cameras on his property to fend off paparazzi and reporters.'

'He's also got a huge great wall between his house and mine, so unless his cameras have X-ray vision, they'll be no use to me.'

'OK, so what about that builder guy on the other side? He must have security cameras to keep his building site safe at night, to ward off would-be thieves from pinching his equipment and materials.'

'That's a comforting thought. I haven't noticed any surveillance cameras before, and Robert and I were keeping an eye out for them when we went into the paddock after dark. Although if he has, I doubt Bolt would share their contents with me. We're hardly best buddies.'

'No one's asking him to share them with you. The police will commandeer any recording for the relevant time. He can't refuse.'

'I doubt he'd have them turned on during the day while he was on site. Or perhaps he was Felicity's attacker, in which case he'd have certainly switched them off to avoid incriminating himself. That would make perfect sense to me.' I shuddered at the thought. 'He had the motive: she was about to force him to down tools. If it's true he's in such debt, every day's work lost will be costing him more than he can afford. Bolt might look small, but those wiry types can be deceptively strong.'

Danny rubbed his chin in thought.

'Plus, he had the element of surprise on his side, if he approached her from behind while she was engrossed in her work,' he said. 'The music she was listening to would have blocked out the sound of his footsteps.'

'And if Magnus was on site this morning – although I didn't see him there – Bolt might easily have sent him away on some fool's errand so he wouldn't be there to witness his attack on Felicity,' I added. 'No wonder he seized on the poison bottle as a possible murder weapon. He was grasping it to distract the police from what he really did. Although it's a bit odd that he should produce a women's scarf to throttle her. I'm sure she wasn't wearing it when I left the shop earlier.'

Danny shrugged.

'Doesn't mean it wasn't in her pocket or her satchel,' he observed. 'Even though it was a warm day, if she had her back to the sun, she might have taken it out to drape round her neck to make sure she didn't get burned.'

'I guess so. Of course, someone who didn't know me might say I'd planted the scarf to divert attention from the fact I'd poisoned her.'

'That's nonsense,' said Danny, taking a sip of his water. 'The marks on her throat and her hoarseness made it obvious someone had strangled her. You have alibis from Suki and Coralie, and anyone else who happened to see you on the high street, to confirm that you weren't there when the attack happened.'

'But the high street was pretty deserted when I went up to the shops. The police would only have my word for it that I left the shop when I said I did. I could have strangled her before I went, when my poison didn't finish her off, and then done a runner to escape detection. You can't deny I had the means and the opportunity, Danny.'

'Stop that nonsense at once,' said Danny, landing a light slap on my thigh. 'You had no motive, and I'm not even sure you had the means. The bottle might have been marked poison, but that doesn't mean it contained anything hazardous. How were the flowers holding up?'

'They looked fine to me, although plants aren't necessarily susceptible to the same poisons as human beings are. Besides, some plants are poisonous in themselves. Foxgloves, for example, contain digitalis. An overdose will stop a human heart.'

Danny grimaced. 'Had you put any foxgloves in the bottle?'

I shook my head. 'No, they'd be too big. I just used flowering culinary herbs like rosemary and chives from the back garden, plus a few sprigs of cow parsley. Not that anyone in their right mind would drink flower water in any case, especially when I'd just given them a delicious glass of sparkling elderflower cordial. But the bottle was in her hand when she keeled over, and the flowers were scattered across the table.'

'Well, there you are, then. She either knocked the bottle over as she fell forward and instinctively grabbed it to stop the flowers falling on the floor, or, as you said just now, seized it as the closest thing she had to a weapon in self-defence against her attacker. Where are the flowers now?'

'The police took the flowers as well as the bottle away for analysis.'

'So, you can't check them to see whether they were OK.'

'No, but let's google cow parsley, as that's the only one that wasn't from the herb patch and not habitually used in cooking. I doubt it can be poisonous, though, considering that cows eat it all the time.'

That made me feel a bit better. But then Danny picked up his phone from the coffee table, typed in a search box, clicked on a link and held the result up to show me. *Cow parsley or hemlock – what's the difference?* read the headline.

I clapped my hand to my mouth in horror. 'I'm sure it was cow parsley,' I said, feeling anything but sure.

'I suppose the police will run tests to be sure. But in the meantime, we can at least check out the likelihood of any of the original poison kept in the bottle affecting her.'

'How?' I was ready to grasp at the slightest glimmer of hope.

'I'll ask my mum,' said Danny.

I was touched by the faith of a man in his forties that his mum was the fount of all knowledge.

'Your mum? What help can she be?'

'Have you forgotten what she does for a living?'

I thought for a moment. I'd only met her a couple of times socially at Danny's previous flat and occasionally when she called into the museum to say hello to him when she was passing.

'A locum pharmacist,' I replied. 'But she's more than that, isn't she? I mean, being a retail pharmacist is a great career in itself, but doesn't she have something to do with the university too?'

Danny nodded proudly. 'Yes, she's an academic, specialising in the history of pharmacy. Let's give her a ring and ask her what sort of poison once might have been sold in a bottle like that. It can only help if we can eliminate possibilities from our investigation.'

He pressed speed dial for her number, then speakerphone. Interrupting her enquiry as to how he was, he cut to the chase, promising to call her later for a general catch-up.

'It could be anything, dear,' she replied. 'But most likely something quite innocuous after being empty and open to the air all this time, and you said Alice had given it a thorough wash before using it as a vase. Until the Arsenic Act of 1851, anyone could march into a pharmacy and buy poisons, and the bottles had to be marked as such. That's why they put the ridges on them – so that they could identify them by touch in dimly lit Victorian houses. But I couldn't tell you now which poison might have been in any particular bottle, not without laboratory analysis of a sample from the interior, and maybe not even then. Even so, if your friend drank straight from it, I doubt she'd come to any harm. There'd be barely a trace. So, I'd say she'll be fine.'

'Unless you believe in homeopathy,' said Danny, and I wished he hadn't.

'Some people swear homoeopathy is effective,' I replied, and I took a deep draught of my wine.

30

AT THE BEDSIDE

It wasn't until the next evening that the police gave me the all-clear to return to the Cotswold Curiosity Shop. Meanwhile, Danny and Martin went to work as usual, and I was left at a loose end. Keen to find out how Felicity was faring, I walked across the city centre to the Royal Infirmary to visit her. I found her sitting up in bed in a small ward, tapping away at her tablet. When she looked up at the sound of my footsteps, she smiled.

'Hi, Alice.' Her voice was still slightly rasping from her strangulation, and the red mark around her neck was now blotched with mauve where the bruising was coming out. 'Thanks for looking after me yesterday.'

At least she didn't seem to suspect me of any foul play towards her. She set her tablet down on the bedside locker and folded her hands on her lap over the blankets.

'I don't suppose you happened to pick up my work phone, did you? It wasn't in my bag with the rest of my things, although I'm sure I had it out on the table alongside my tablet. I had it on the table so I could check texts from the office while I was typing up my report.'

I shook my head. 'Sorry, I didn't see it. I wonder whether someone pinched it in the melee?'

'The melee? What melee? Who else was around? The last person I remember seeing was you, going off up the road.'

I hoped she hadn't told the police that.

'And then that posh bloke who called the ambulance,' she continued, wrinkling her nose. 'I wouldn't put him down as a petty thief. I got the impression that he's loaded.'

'That's true. He lives in the biggest house in Little Pride. If you believe the village grapevine, he'd be a smoother operator than the average phone thief. He's actually a retired spy.'

Her eyes widened. 'You've got a bit of everything in Little Pride, haven't you?'

I grinned. 'And in my shop too. But I tell you what, if anyone was going to take advantage of your unconscious state to steal some tech equipment, surely they'd have taken your tablet? That must be worth more than your phone on the black market.'

She nodded. 'Yes, but I'd taken site photos on my phone rather on my tablet, so perhaps they were after the incriminating photos rather than just some random bit of tech kit to sell on for cash.'

Our eyes locked in a moment of recognition. I was the first to speak.

'So you think whoever stole the phone was planning to delete the photographic evidence of the mosaic from your phone?'

'Yes. But what they didn't know was that I didn't take the pictures of the mosaic on my work phone,' said Felicity. 'I always use my personal phone for site photography because it has a much better camera. While I was writing up my report, my own phone was safely stashed in my handbag. It also automatically uploads new photos to the cloud, so even if they'd stolen the right phone – my personal one – they couldn't have got rid of the evidence.'

'So there's the motive for attacking you,' I suggested. 'They weren't really trying to do you serious harm, just to frighten you off while they deleted your evidence of the mosaic. They might also have hoped the disruption might also buy them time to clear all trace of the mosaic from the paddock.'

Her face fell.

'That chimes with the string of anonymous messages I've received on my work email account this morning.' Her voice fell to almost a whisper. 'I've never had anything like it before.'

She reached for her tablet, opened the email menu, and handed it to me. I gasped as I read the vile stream of threats against her safety, her children and her cat if she didn't stop her investigations at local building sites. The old paddock wasn't mentioned but given the timing, it didn't take a genius to make the connection.

'This is atrocious,' I said. 'You must show this to the police straight away.'

She sank back against the pillows.

'I know.' Her voice took on a childlike vulnerability. 'And to my line manager at the council. I almost deleted the messages and blocked the sender, but I didn't want to destroy evidence before I'd done that. I'll also show them to the council's IT manager as soon as I get out of here, which they tell me should be later today after the doctor's ward rounds. But first I'm going to take advantage of the unexpected bed rest and have a little nap.'

Her eyelids were drooping already, and as I got up from the bedside chair, her eyes closed.

'I'm so tired, Alice, I can't tell you.'

'Yes, get some rest, Felicity,' I said. 'And if the police interview me before they get to you, do I have your permission to tell them about those awful messages? They might be able to track the sender.'

But she was already asleep.

31

SAFE AS HOUSES

My car was still in the garage pending delivery of new parts, and Danny had kindly volunteered to drive me home in Martin's car once they had both finished work. On the journey, I relayed to him what I'd learned from my visit to Felicity.

'Then the phone thief is an idiot,' he declared as we joined the motorway.

'Why do you say that?' I asked.

'Because it's obvious that a professional like her will automatically save their photos to the cloud.'

'So, pinching the phone won't have served any purpose,' I surmised.

'Except perhaps to give the culprit a false sense of security. Whoever they are must be pretty stupid, or not very tech-aware.'

'That's more evidence that it might have been Bolt, if you ask me,' I said. 'Same goes for the threatening messages. It's hardly subtle. Yet how could even Bolt be so brazen as to attack Felicity in broad daylight? Bolt may not be the sharpest blade in the Swiss Army knife, but I don't believe even he would be that stupid.'

Danny laughed. 'Because it was the only chance he'd have to

frighten her off? Because he was desperate? It sounds from what you've said as if he's on the brink of bankruptcy. With a clear view up and down the high street, he might have thought he had a golden opportunity that might not come again.'

Without thinking, I put my hand to my throat. 'You mean you think he meant to – er – finish the job?'

'To kill her?' he asked. 'Who knows? Perhaps he just wanted to frighten her off, leaving him to carry on with his precious development.' He pulled up on the road outside my shop. 'Now, before I drop you off, are you sure you're OK to stay in the cottage on your own? I can spend the night if you like.'

It was a tempting offer, but I'd sensed when Martin had said goodbye to me at their flat that he was glad to see the back of me. He clearly didn't want me to impose on another of their evenings together.

'That's very kind, Danny, but I couldn't possibly ask you to do that. Besides, you've got work tomorrow, and you haven't got any overnight things. It's not as if a pair of my pyjamas would fit you.'

He smirked, producing a toothbrush from his back pocket. 'I also sneaked a change of clothes into the boot when you and Martin weren't looking, just after you'd put your overnight bag in there. I don't mind staying, Alice, honest.'

I shook my head. I didn't want to get him into trouble with Martin. Even though I didn't like Martin, I didn't want to upset their relationship.

'No, I'll be OK, Danny, really. Bolt has already gone home for the night, and I've no one else in the village to fear. Besides, I can always give Robert Praed next door a shout if I'm nervous, or Andrew Gloster. He's been very kind to me since I moved here, and he was the very first friend I made in Little Pride.'

Danny pulled a face. He hadn't taken to either of them.

'So don't worry about me. I'll be fine. Now, you get on home to

Martin.' I tried to make light of my situation. 'If I'm worried, I'll just invite old Maudie Frampton round to keep attackers at bay with her hobnailed boots.'

Danny sighed. 'OK, if you're sure. But remember you can always phone me, day or night, and I'll be here as fast as the speed limit allows me.'

When I leaned over to plant a thank-you kiss on his cheek, he slid his hand round my shoulders and pulled me close for a hug.

All the same, as I marched up the path, swinging my bag, trying to look defiant, I was perturbed to see Andrew and Bolt at the far corner of the paddock, deep in conversation. So, the developer hadn't gone home yet after all. Still, at least I'd be safe while Andrew was around. I left them to their conflab and headed indoors.

* * *

I'd not slept well at Danny and Martin's flat after the upset of the previous day, but only when I had settled down in my dining room with a cup of bedtime cocoa did I realise how weary I was. It must have been the earliest I'd been to bed for years, because as I closed my bedroom shutters before snuggling down beneath the duvet, the sky was not quite dark.

All was silent, apart from the clanging of a spade against the hardened soil next door. I imagined Bolt was still in search of lost gold and smiled to myself.

Either that or he could no longer afford to pay Magnus and was having to break the ground for the rest of the development all by himself. That would mean labouring all hours if he was working alone. What a massive task that would be. No wonder he was burning the not-quite-midnight oil.

As I drifted off to sleep, my last conscious thought was to wonder where Magnus was now.

Next morning, I was just about to make my breakfast when there was a knock at the door. I hesitated. If it was Bolt coming to hurl more abuse and threats at me, I didn't want to open it. He had no rights over me, and I wasn't going to submit to his bullying. On the other hand, my visitor might be a more welcome one – Andrew, or even Robert. I dashed up the stairs and peered down from the front bedroom window to be sure.

To my relief, it was Coralie, holding a wooden trug of runner beans and sweet peas. I rapped on the window to attract her attention, smiling and waving, relieved to see a friendly presence. Then I ran down the stairs and flung the front door open, beckoning her inside.

'For you!' she announced, holding out the trug as she stepped over the threshold. 'Well, the contents, anyway. I stupidly picked more than I'm likely to sell today and there's no fridge in my tiny house. So, I thought I'd bring them round to lift your spirits. Suki told me this morning about the nightmare you had yesterday with that council lady, and I thought you might need cheering up.' She bit her lip. 'OK, I confess, I also wanted to hear your side of the story rather than trusting the jungle drums.'

I appreciated her honesty and invited her to follow me through to the dining room for a cup of tea and some cake.

'I haven't got my first client until midday, but shouldn't you be opening your shop now? It's gone ten.'

I hesitated. Everyone had said I could dictate my own opening hours, and what I'd had printed in the *Parish News* was hardly law. But it seemed like a good idea to open at the scheduled time to show I was undaunted by the events of the last twenty-four hours. It would also help my reputation if people saw Coralie enjoying a drink on my tea terrace.

I sent her out to sit at one of the tea tables while I prepared coffee and cake for us. I made a point of sitting with my back to the paddock so that there'd be less chance of Bolt hearing what I was saying to her.

'So do you think there really are ancient Roman tiles on his site?' Coralie asked in a low voice.

'That's for Felicity to say once she's had them scientifically certified, but she is pretty sure they are. Then it's for her to decide whether to halt the development for further investigation or allow it to go ahead.'

Coralie nodded towards the paddock behind me.

'It looks like she might already have told him to down tools. All his equipment is standing idle. He's just digging away with an old-fashioned spade all by himself.' She laughed. 'Where are his workers? Or rather, worker? Sorry, Barnaby.' She raised her eyes heavenward for a moment.

'I'm thinking he hasn't paid Magnus, and he's on strike.'

'That'll slow his build down.' Coralie leaned towards me and lowered her voice. 'I cut Andrew's hair last week, and he told me Bolt's desperate for cash. He reckons he's taken on too many projects too fast and has had to borrow heavily to be able to fund the paddock development. So that would stack up with him being unable to pay Magnus or any other labourers.'

'So, finding a crock of Roman gold would ease his way.'

'Don't tell me he's found gold there as well as mosaic tiles?'

'Not that he's letting on, and I should think he'd be highly unlikely to. But Felicity piqued his greed by mentioning the Tetbury hoard, which was dug up in 2010. Two earthenware pots contained over a quarter of a million pounds' worth of Roman gold coins.'

'That would be a neat answer to his financial crisis,' said Coralie. 'Maybe we should have a whip-round in the pub and buy him a metal detector.' She glanced up at the sky. 'I think I just felt a drop of rain. That'll do my beans good. By the way, all this makes me wonder now about a bag of tiny tiles Nell Little gave me in payment for her last hairdo. She was matey with the farmer who owned the paddock before Bolt bought the land, so I bet he gave them to her.'

'Have you still got the bag of tiles?' I asked, my hopes rising until she shook her head.

'No, I used them to make a teapot stand. I sold it last summer for a fiver. I was quite pleased at the time, as the materials had cost me nothing, but if you're right about them being Roman, my customer got the better bargain. I wish I could remember who I sold it to. Still, best not to fret over things you can't fix. Nell might have got them from somewhere completely different. Or I might have misremembered them. They could have been modern and not worth anything at all.'

I pushed the last few cake crumbs around my plate, making a neat pile. 'If only Nell Little were still alive, we could ask her. An extra piece of evidence that the paddock contains ancient Roman artefacts would be handy at this stage. I'm sure Bolt will use every trick in the book to wriggle out of Felicity's holding order.'

Coralie banged her cup with a clatter onto the saucer. 'But you can talk to Nell Little any time you like.'

'Don't tell me you're a clairvoyant as well as all your other talents?' That wouldn't have surprised me, but I didn't fancy being inveigled into a séance. Besides, evidence from beyond Nell's grave would hardly stand up in court.

The supernatural had made me anxious ever since I'd experimented with a Ouija board with some schoolfriends on a sleepover. We'd had some very odd messages from my friend's late great uncle. Of course, I'd realised years later that one of the other girls had been first to put her forefinger on the upturned cup every time we interrogated the board, and that she must have been controlling its movement.

'Medium, schmedium,' declared Coralie with a laugh. 'Whatever made you think Nell Little is no longer in the land of the living? She's alive and well in the old folks' home over at Wendlebury Barrow.'

'Where's that? Is it far from here?'

The name was familiar. Miles Swansong had suggested a viewing at a cottage in that village, but I didn't bother as I'd already lost my heart to the Cotswold Curiosity Shop.

'Twenty minutes by car. Provided you give the care home advance notice, I'm sure they'll let you visit her. She's a sociable old soul and still got all her marbles. She's just too frail physically to live on her own these days.'

I threw my hands in the air, nearly sending the tea table flying.

'Why did nobody tell me before?' I cried. 'Everyone's talked about her in such tragic tones that I assumed she'd met a terrible end. I didn't like to ask the details for fear of upsetting anyone. Not least myself, because I assumed she had met her grim death in my cottage.'

Coralie tipped her chair onto its two back legs as she laughed.

'You must tell that to Nell. She'll be highly amused.' She glanced at her watch. 'Anyway, I must dash, or Maudie Frampton will be on my doorstep before I can open up. Let me know how you get on with Nell Little and give her a big hug from me.'

It was only when she scooped up her patchwork tote bag from the back of her chair that I noticed hanging in a bow from the handle a tie-dyed scarf almost exactly like Felicity's.

32

LITTLE NELL

Before I opened the shop next morning, in the continuing absence of my own car and of any buses, I decided to phone Andrew to try to blag a lift to Wendlebury Barrow. After all, there was a potential news story in it for his magazine if Nell Little was able to remember helpful details about what might lie beneath the paddock. I leaned my back against the trade counter as I waited for him to pick up, trying to decide whether I had the energy to paint the shelves that lined the back wall of the shop.

To my surprise, Andrew was not only unwilling to visit Nell but critical of the very idea.

'Sorry, Alice, Nell Little is hardly a reliable witness. She'd become very forgetful in her last few months at the shop, opening in the middle of the night or neglecting to lock up at the end of the day. You can't expect her to remember anything about individual stock items when she stocked so many goods over the years, sourced from all and sundry. It would be unkind even to ask her. Being unable to remember might cause her distress and embarrassment. If I were you, I'd leave her in peace and let her keep her dignity while she's in the final room.'

From my experience of chatting with elderly visitors in the museum, I thought he was being excessively judgemental.

'Yes, but even if old people have trouble with their short-term memories, they often remember things from long ago very well indeed.'

He tried to make a joke of it. 'Yes, but not from the ancient Roman past.'

I didn't laugh.

'Anyway, I'm not in a fit state to take you just now. I'm in my gardening clothes. I'm making the most of this dry spell to catch up with some garden maintenance before the weather breaks. Don't you know there's a storm due in the next day or two? If you're looking for something to fill your time, you'd be better off tending your garden rather than going off on some wild goose chase. If you think your garden's overgrown now, just wait until after the downpour. Within a day or two, it'll be like trying to cut back triffids.'

A simple no would have done, I thought, but didn't say for fear of antagonising him further. He hadn't yet published his report on the grand reopening of the Cotswold Curiosity Shop, and there was still time for him to change it for the worse before the next issue of the *Little Pride Parish News* came out.

Then another idea occurred to me: perhaps he'd had an early sundowner, a habit he might have acquired in his service overseas and didn't like to admit he'd be over the limit for driving. Still waiting to hear my blood test results from the police, I could understand how he felt. I decided not to press him any further.

As I ended the call, I turned round and realised that while I was speaking, Robert had come into the shop.

'Never trust a person who makes more than one excuse when you ask them to do something,' advised Robert with a wry smile. My mobile was on speakerphone, and he must have heard every word. 'By the way, I'll be at a loose end when you shut up your shop tonight. I'm happy to run you over to Wendlebury Barrow if you like. It's not one of my Tilly days, which is just as well, because she'd be pestering me to take her into the village bookshop and tea room, Hector's House, and buy her a book.'

The fond twinkle in his eye told me that Tilly would never be short of reading matter while in her grandfather's care.

'That's a good place to offload any unwanted books, by the way. Hector and Sophie run a decent second-hand book department above the main bookshop and tea room.'

I'd been wondering why there were no books in the Cotswold Curiosity Shop. Perhaps Nell hadn't wanted to be in competition with Hector's House. The more I found out about her, the more I liked and respected her.

True to his word, Robert pulled up outside the Cotswold Curiosity Shop in his dark-green Morgan just as I was turning my *Open* sign to *Closed* at five o'clock. The top of the car was folded back to make the most of the early-evening sunshine. As I slid into the passenger seat, Robert pointed to a cluster of bright, floral hair scrunchies on the dashboard.

'Feel free to borrow one of Tilly's hair thingies if you want to keep your lovely locks tidy along the way. Coralie told me she'd cut your hair shorter when you moved in – I had mine done the other day too – but you'll find it's still long enough to get tangled in the wind.'

I took his advice and chose a rose-patterned velvet one. He glanced at me out of the corner of his eye as I gathered my hair back.

'Suits you,' he said.

Feeling a little self-conscious now, I smiled politely before changing the subject.

'Robert, how well do you know Nell Little?' I sat back in the soft, caramel leather seat, resting my left elbow on the door's sill.

'Only ever since I was Tilly's age.'

'So not long at all, then?' I teased.

'Of course, there have been long periods when I haven't seen her, because my parents sold my old childhood home when I was at university and retired to a bungalow in West Wales. But when I bought it back a few years ago, Nell still remembered me. She and my mother were good friends.'

He turned off the main road onto a winding, leafy lane. On either side, fields of apple-green wheat rippled in the breeze.

'What about Nell's family? Does she have any?'

'No. She was the only child. Mr and Mrs Littlewood died in the 1980s, and they had both been only children too. No wonder Nell stayed on in Little Pride to take over their shop, where everyone knew her. I don't think she was ever lonely.'

'Hang on, rewind a moment. Did you call her parents the Little-woods? Don't tell me I've been calling her the wrong name all this time?'

He grinned. 'Yes, sorry, it's another village thing. Barely anyone is known by their given name around here. I'm surprised your lawyer didn't tell you her full name when he was doing your conveyancing.'

I was beyond being surprised by anything my lawyer did.

'We just called her Little for short, not least because she was petite. Then when she had the sign above her shop repainted to reflect the change of ownership after her parents died, she shortened her given name, Eleanor, to Nell, to be reminiscent of Charles Dickens' famous novel *The Old Curiosity Shop*.'

'But Little Nell dies young in the novel. Didn't that put her off? Nominative determinism and all that.'

Robert shrugged. 'She just gave priority to making the shop a success. Considering she left school at fourteen, and she took the shop over long before the Internet and online searches were invented, Nell was a savvy marketer, way ahead of her time.'

I had to agree.

* * *

The minute I met Nell, I realised why everyone called her Little. I know people tend to shrink with age, but she was miniscule, though mighty in spirit and character.

One of the carers, a pleasant young woman in her twenties, showed us into her room. Nell was sitting beside a bay window with a grand view of the well-kept garden, her small, pink fingers wrapped around a floral-patterned teacup. With her beady, brown eyes and her tiny hands, she reminded me of a Beatrix Potter illustration from *The Tale of Two Bad Mice*.

Nell recognised Robert at once and beckoned him to bend down to plant a kiss on her cheek. After he had introduced me, and I'd shaken her delicate hand with care, she was quick to ask about the welfare of her old shop. When I told her I'd kept the name and had barely changed the interior beyond cleaning and tidying, she took to me straight away and told me she'd be very willing to answer any questions. That was a stroke of luck.

Rather than risk tarnishing her goodwill by ploughing straight into the sensitive issue of the mosaic tiles, I took the opportunity to ask a few practical questions about the running of the shop, such as recommendations for how to keep it ticking over outside of the tourist season and what she used to do there for Christmas.

When her eyelids dipped for a moment, I realised my barrage of questions was tiring her, so I got to the point.

'Did anyone ever bring you any loose mosaic tiles to sell in your shop, Nell?'

She closed her eyes and tapped her thin lower lip with a bony forefinger while she considered. When her eyes sprang open, they were bright and alert.

'Yes, the old fellow next door used to do so from time to time. What was his name? Neddy, that was it. Neddy Jones was the gentleman who owned the donkey paddock in those days.'

Robert suppressed a smile. 'Before you ask, Alice, no, his name wasn't really Neddy. It was Ivor.'

I shook my head in disbelief. Wasn't anyone known by their real names in Little Pride? It must make the place a gift to Andrew Gloster, if the rumours about hiding from his past as a spy were true.

I quickly established we were not at cross purposes – that these were Roman tesserae we were talking about, not just shards of more recent china.

'Do you know where he got them from?' I asked, hopefully.

'From the paddock, whenever he was breaking soil to plant a new shrub or tree,' Nell recalled. 'He was a kind man with the same gentle demeanour as his beasts, and he said I could have as many of the little fragments as I liked. But truth be told, I wasn't that bothered. I didn't think my customers would be either. They tended to be after old-fashioned china like my mother and grandmother had, the sort with a pretty picture on it, like willow pattern or Delft rather than plain, dull colours. So, after a bucket or two, I said enough is enough, and he left the rest of them in the ground for want of anything better to do with them.'

I exchanged knowing looks with Robert. This all stacked up.

'Besides, I don't see the point in keeping really old things present company excepted.' She gave a shrill giggle. 'Life's for the living, my dears. No need to resurrect the dead.'

'No, but finds from antiquity will always be of interest to archaeologists,' I said gently. I went on to explain my theory about buried tesserae being evidence of an ancient Roman mosaic workshop in the paddock. I also told her Felicity's theory that behind the site of the old stable there had once been a strip villa with a mosaic floor, or even something larger scale, which only a controlled archaeological excavation could confirm or rule out.

Nell considered for a moment.

'Well, I did hear tell of something along those lines when I was a girl. Our schoolmaster said that his grandfather had once owned the paddock and much else of the village. His old grandpa reckoned there had once been a Roman settlement here, but no one took much notice in those days. We were too busy surviving the present, what with two generations of village boys going off to the war never to return, God rest their souls. But it makes sense that a quarry would have been a draw to Romans, with all that stone ready for the taking – just what they needed to build their villas. Most of the houses around here were built from locally quarried stone, including both of yours, my dears.'

It was ironic that Nell was the first villager to refer to the place as mine rather than hers.

'I had no idea there had once been a quarry in Little Pride,' I said. 'I haven't noticed any quarry dust or the associated noise this side of the quarries by Chipping Sodbury.'

'Why, of course there was a quarry here. Where do you think Little Pride got its name? Or has that rogue Andrew Gloster stopped putting the village history in every issue of the *Little Pride Parish News*? I spelled it all out there, and I told him to keep it in when he insisted on taking it over from me as editor. Not that I'd expect that chump to do what I told him. Too arrogant by half.'

This was a powerful reminder that she hadn't always been this old and infirm. Even the Roman mosaics had once been shiny and new.

'I gave in against my better judgement,' she continued, with a reproachful shake of her head. 'The wretch appealed to the parish council to be allowed to take it off my hands, claiming I was no longer up to it.'

The faintest frown lines clouded her porcelain brow, but I sensed the kind old soul had long forgiven him. It might even have come as a relief at the time. From the one issue I'd seen so far, assembling it every month must be a mammoth task for any individual.

'I'm sorry to hear that,' I began.

She waved my sympathy away. 'My point is, if he'd left my village history in the parish news, you'd have known that Little Pride is a corruption of Little Praeda. Praeda is Latin for quarry. Ours was the smaller of the two local quarries. The larger was at Great Pride a couple of miles west. Back in the twenties, the council decided to change the names from the original Latin, replacing Praeda with Pride. In fact, Little Pride was originally Praeda Parva, meaning small, and Great Pride was Praeda Magna, which you don't need me to translate.'

'What a bizarre decision,' I replied. 'The original names were much prettier. Why on earth did they change them?'

Nell clasped her tiny hands in her lap. 'They were hoping to attract the new breed of leisure motorists who pottered down here from the towns and cities on high days and holidays. They were afeard such visitors wouldn't be able to spell the old-fashioned names so wouldn't find them on their maps. My parents and the other ordinary folk of their generation always mourned the change, and younger folk don't even seem to know about it. You'd be hard pressed now, of course, to guess the quarry was there. It's long since fallen into disuse, and it's been mostly grassed over for years. But if you look for it, you can spot the straight edges beneath the undergrowth where the stone was cut out in great blocks. You can still spot the name here and there too. The war memorial still bears the old name, because changing it to Little Pride would have shown a shocking disrespect for our boys' sacrifice.'

'Alice, haven't you ever wondered why the village pub was called The Quarrymen's Arms?' asked Robert, smiling.

'It does explain the lump hammer on the primary school badge.' I gave a wry smile. 'Now I can see that it represents what must have once been the two main sources of employment in the village, quarrying and farming, showing the traditional tools of the trade.' I clapped my hand to my cheek at my own stupidity. 'There was me thinking the school had some kind of communist leaning with its hammer and sickle emblem.'

The corners of Nell's mouth twitched.

'My dear, if you're going to live in the country, it's time you learned the difference between a sickle and a scythe.' She leaned back a little in her armchair, before adding, 'I'm afraid that little trip down memory lane has rather exhausted me.'

We took the hint, thanked her profusely for her time, and got up to leave.

'Come again anytime, my dears. It's not every day I get to chat to such a pleasant young couple. And I'm glad to see you're keeping company again, young Bobby.'

As we headed for the door, Robert laughed a little self-consciously. I wasn't sure which we found more amusing, the notion that at our age we could pass for young, or that she taken us to be a couple. Either way, we now had another, living, witness that Roman remains had previously been found in the paddock. This could only strengthen our case.

'By the way, my dear,' said Nell, as I turned to wave before closing the door, 'I'm so pleased you have such a suitable name to take over my shop. It's high time that old sign was repainted. From now on, why don't you call it Alice's Cotswold Curiosity Shop? The name will make people think of the Sheep's Shop in *Through the Looking Glass and What Alice Found There*, and who doesn't love Lewis Carroll's Alice?'

Nell may not have realised, but she'd just given me a valuable gift.

33

ENTRENCHED THINKING

When we arrived back at Little Pride, Robert swung the Morgan through the open wrought-iron gates of his house.

'This feels like cause for celebration, Alice,' he said as we climbed out of the car.

'Aren't you being a little premature?' I replied. 'The council hasn't yet put a stop to Bolt's building project. He could still bribe or wheedle his way around them, especially in the absence of poor Felicity.'

Robert bent over to raise the Morgan's top for the night. 'I wasn't talking about that. I meant getting Nell's blessing to rename the shop as your own.'

I brightened a little. 'Yes, it is rather, isn't it? I hadn't even thought of doing that until she suggested it, but I'm very glad she did. Maybe then people will stop referring to me living in Nell's house.'

Robert raised his eyebrows. 'It'll be a step in the right direction anyway. So, do you fancy a drink to celebrate? Prosecco in my garden? There's a bottle chilling in the fridge.'

'That does sound appealing,' I admitted. 'But first things first.

Will you give me a minute to call Felicity about our visit to Nell? I wouldn't mind putting a comb through my hair either. Tilly's scrunchie was a help, but my hair feels like I've been turning cartwheels in a wind tunnel.'

Robert selected his house key from a large bunch on his key ring. 'Sure. While I'm waiting, I'll rummage through my larder for some nibbles for us to share. I'll leave the front door on the latch for you to let yourself in when you're ready.'

As I strolled back to my cottage, I was feeling so empowered by Nell's evidence that when I saw Terence Bolt wielding a spade on a fresh patch of soil, I called a cheery 'good evening' to him. That surprised him.

'Found any Roman gold yet, Mr Bolt?' I added, which made him snarl a reply that I couldn't quite catch. That was probably just as well.

As I brushed my hair in the reflection of an old, gilt-framed mirror in the shop, I wondered what might happen if Bolt really did find any other heritage treasure. It would make front-page headlines on the *Little Pride Parish News* for sure.

That prompted me to think of Andrew Gloster. I was in a benevolent frame of mind, buoyed up by the prospect of sipping fizz in the congenial Robert's back garden, seeing behind its high wall for the first time.

After all, Andrew had been the first person I'd met in the village, and he had seemed so supportive to me and my little business venture. If it hadn't been for his advice and the free advertisement in the *Parish News*, I might now be seriously considering selling the Cotswold Curiosity Shop to the wretched Bolt, if indeed he could rustle up the necessary funds. But what did I really know about Andrew beyond that? Only the rumours about his past as a spy. These were hardly great character references.

My conscience demanded that before I decamped to Robert'

garden, I should bring Andrew up to speed on our findings. Gifting him the scoop for the *Little Pride Parish News* over the local paper should keep him onside for my shop for ever more. I stepped out into the garden to get a decent phone signal. When Andrew didn't pick up, I left a voicemail asking him to call me back as soon as possible so I could tell him exciting news about the paddock.

I tapped in a quick text to Robert to say I was still trying to get hold of Andrew, and Robert immediately replied with an emoji of champagne glasses being clinked together for cheers.

When Andrew didn't return my call, I assumed he had left his phone indoors while gardening. I left another voicemail saying I'd pop round to tell him my news in person and strode up the high street to the Big House. His Range Rover was on the drive, but there was no answer when I rang the old-fashioned bellpull at the front door. However, I could hear something mechanical churning away behind the house. If Andrew was in the garden, he wouldn't hear the doorbell over that racket.

The Big House was a detached property. The wide passage at one side, leading to the back garden, was shaded by a boundary wall even higher than Robert's. I marched down the passage, calling Andrew's name. I guessed he was doing a bit of construction work of his own, laying a new patio or something like that. Perhaps that noise was coming from a cement mixer. No wonder he'd been a bit touchy when I called him earlier. You had to work fast with cement, and he would have been cross to have to stop in the middle of such a big job to answer his phone.

As I reached the back of the house, my smile of greeting froze, for there in front of me was a huge rectangle of cleared lawn. On three side lay piles of freshly dug earth. Behind them were stacked neatly cut turves. After the cool shade of the passage, I had to shield my eyes with my hand as I adjusted to bright sunshine reflecting off a large stone patio. At the far end of the garden, I spotted Andrew with his back to me. Between us stretched a narrow, deeply rutted track, apparently caused by the wheelbarrow now at his side. On top of the wheelbarrow lay what looked like a large square door mat, or at least a square of something with a brown edge the thickness of a door mat. As Andrew grasped the handles of the wheelbarrow to slide the doormat onto the cleared rectangle, the cement mixer cut out, and the door of a nearby stone shed swung open to reveal Magnus with the cement mixer's plug in his hand. He called out to Andrew.

'So that's the last piece, mate. Fantastic! I'll be back first thing tomorrow to shovel the earth back over it, and then we can relay the lawn by the end of the day.'

I stepped back into the shadows at the side of the house, my hand over my mouth to conceal my gasp.

Magnus! He seemed as hale and hearty as ever, so he can't have been off sick. He certainly wasn't on strike, judging by the spatters of mud and cement across his glistening bare chest. Perhaps he had lied to Bolt about a supposed illness in order to moonlight for Andrew. Maybe Andrew had made him a better offer, or simply offered him cash in hand, which Bolt couldn't possibly match in his current financial state. For a moment I almost felt sorry for Bolt, all alone at the paddock trying to build a new estate single-handed.

Unsure what I'd say to Magnus or Andrew if they noticed me, I decided the safest bet was to flee. It would have been embarrassing to be caught up in their subterfuge.

Now that the cement mixer was silent, I was conscious of every move I made. I didn't want to announce my presence with the crunch of gravel underfoot. I retreated on tiptoe, watching every footfall to pick the least gravelly spot.

Then I stopped altogether at the sight of a flash of blue amid the butterscotch pebbles. Stooping for closer inspection, I discovered some blue tesserae attached to some other pieces of stone almos indistinguishable from the gravel. As I picked up the blue stones, they brought with them a grid of about thirty pieces cemented together on top of some binding material. All in all, it was far heavier than I anticipated, and I had to support it with the palm of my other hand to stop it falling and landing noisily on the ground.

At first glance, I thought, *What's one of Coralie's coasters doing here?*

Then I realised the blue colours were solid, not the blue and white of willow pattern. What I'd taken for pieces of gravel were small cubes of terracotta, bound together with the blue tiles with some sort of ancient tile cement. As grains of dirt clinging to the underside of this fragment of mosaic tickled my palm, I realised it was part of an ancient Roman floor, a floor that, with the help of Magnus, Andrew was now re-laying in a pit in his own back garden and preparing to conceal.

What on earth was he thinking? To stage a surprise reveal at a later date, in hope of passing it off as his own? To keep it hidden for as long as he pleased, as some kind of pension? I knew that found mosaics had often been reburied to preserve them in situ, but this one, although ancient, was being newly installed.

If he'd bought it from Bolt, Bolt would have been only too pleased to have it removed so that he could carry on with his build. Or perhaps, in league with Magnus, working through the night, and transporting it in the back of his Range Rover, he'd stolen it. Either way, it would mean Bolt's building project could continue, and he could repay his debts.

I guessed Magnus would have no real idea of the significance of what he was doing. He was probably following paid orders, whether from Bolt or Andrew or both. Perhaps he even thought he was doing a good thing by preserving the mosaic rather than chucking in on the skip, as Bolt had instructed Barnaby to do with his other subterranean finds. But Andrew must surely have realised the enormity of the heritage crime he was committing, whether or not he was in collusion with Bolt.

I covered the mosaic segment with my other hand, intent on keeping it safe and out of sight. It must have fallen off the wheel-barrow as they transported it from Andrew's Range Rover to the end of the garden. I winced. Moving and relocating a Roman mosaic was specialist work, not something to be done by a general jobbing labourer. I needed to put a stop to their vandalism now before they could do even more damage.

Taking a deep breath, I strode out of the shadows, across the patio and onto the lawn. Magnus saw me first, dropping his spade in surprise.

As the spade clanged onto the stonework below, Andrew spun round, wide eyed. As soon as he saw me, he scowled, raising his spade to shoulder height. I forced an innocent smile. As I marched closer, I saw before me, lying at the bottom of the rectangular trench, a whole mosaic floor in the colours familiar from the stash of tesserae Barnaby had uncovered.

Or rather a badly assembled, almost-whole mosaic. The floor had been inexpertly cut into segments for ease of transport, and they had re-laid it here like so many carpet tiles. Immediately, I spotted two segments put in the wrong way round, making a horse's leg protrude from its back. But at least the floor was complete, all except a small, square hole towards the centre, which exactly matched the piece now concealed between my cupped hands.

'Goodness, Andrew, isn't it frustrating when you complete a jigsaw only to find the last piece is missing?' I said sweetly, raising my upper hand to reveal the missing mosaic fragment on my palm.

Then I slid the fragment into my jacket pocket out of his reach and rubbed my hands together to brush off the surplus soil.

Andrew and Magnus stared at each other for a moment. I took advantage of their apparent bewilderment and made a run for it. As

I charged down the passage, I was conscious that Andrew had launched himself after me from the far end of the lawn. I didn't look to see whether he was still wielding that spade.

As I turned the corner of the front of the house, I barged straight into an unexpected obstacle. At first, I feared it was another of Andrew's henchmen – sorry, labourers. As soon as we collided, my face buried in his chest, I leaped back, fearful that he would grab me and haul me into the back garden, away from public view. If there was still wet cement in that mixer, perhaps it would be me that archaeologists of the future would be uncovering alongside the re-sited Roman mosaic. They would be puzzled as to why my remains didn't match the carbon-dating of the mosaic.

Then to my relief I realised it was Robert Praed's hands on my shoulders, steadying me as I wobbled. Instinctively, I leaned in, and he hugged me to him. His crisp, linen shirt smelled of line-dried washing.

'Alice, are you OK?' Robert was saying. 'I was worried about you after I heard you leaving voicemail messages for Andrew, so I thought I'd pop up here myself to check nothing was wrong. I hope you don't think I'm stalking you. I'll just go home if you like.'

I was too shocked to give a coherent reply, but Robert got his answer when Andrew careered around the corner and into the passage, wielding his spade aloft like a weapon.

'What on earth's going on, Gloster?' Robert cried.

Andrew lowered the spade and leaned on it, as if trying to look innocent.

'Just get me out of here and I'll tell you,' I whispered against Robert's chest.

Robert had driven up for the sake of speed, parking on Andrew's gravel drive. We dashed to his car, leaped into the seats and, without pausing to fasten our safety belts, we circled the fountain, sped out through the open gates and onto the high street, which was thankfully clear of pedestrians.

We didn't speak until we were safely parked on his drive and had fastened his gates behind us. But even in the silence, I felt almost deafened by a pounding in my ears, my pulse racing as the adrenaline coursed through my body.

With his arm around my shoulders, Robert let me gently into his house, through the entrance hall, and onto a conker-brown leather Chesterfield in his front room. I was glad it faced the bay window overlooking the drive, so I could be sure Andrew and Magnus hadn't followed us.

Robert crossed the room to open a gleaming Art Deco cocktail cabinet, poured a couple of glasses of sweet sherry, and pressed one into my hand. I took a couple of sips, then set it down on the vast oak coffee table neatly stacked with back issues of *Cotswold Life*.

I patted my jacket pocket to make sure my evidence was still there before slipping my hand inside and pulling out the fragment of mosaic floor.

'We were right,' I said at last, my voice hoarse. 'There *is* a mosaic floor in the paddock behind where the stable used to be. Or rather, there was. Between them, Andrew and Magnus have rather clumsily removed the whole thing to Andrew's back garden. I'm not sure Bolt even knows. I think he's been too focused on finding Little Pride's answer to the Tetbury hoard of gold. Goodness knows what damage they've done to the floor in the process, but this is a piece of it. It must have dropped off as they removed it.'

Robert blinked as if in disbelief. 'How on earth did they manage that? It must weigh a ton.'

'Absolutely,' I replied. 'This square fragment is heavy enough. They wouldn't have been able to lift it all at once, but they've sliced it into more manageable squares, like a traybake of chocolate brownies. Then they must have loaded it piece by piece into

Andrew's Range Rover and wheelbarrowed it section by section from Andrew's drive to his back garden, where they had the right-sized trench already cut, and turves at the ready to conceal their theft.'

'Presumably, Andrew was planning to rebury it and miraculously discover it at a later date, hoping for either financial reward or attention. He does like attention.'

'Magnus, Bolt's labourer, is as strong as a gorilla, so Andrew must have bribed him or otherwise persuaded him to do the heavy lifting. I bet he'd be clueless about ancient history and the strict laws on preserving heritage finds. I guess this also explains why he's been absent from the paddock recently. During the daytime, he must have been sleeping off his unofficial night shift. I think he's been sneaking back to the paddock after dark and removing the mosaic by stealth.'

'I'm surprised the noise of his nocturnal excavations didn't wake you up,' said Robert.

I hesitated. 'Actually, I'm just a very deep sleeper. My mum used to say I slept like the dead.'

I grimaced, and Robert chuckled.

'Bolt must have been glad to get the mosaic off his land so he could press on with his development,' he went on. 'But there's no excuse for Andrew. He must have known the significance of this find.'

'If not, Felicity Stride would have enlightened him. Oh, my.' My hand shot to my mouth. 'Which means that Andrew must be prime suspect for trying to silence her by attacking her on my tea terrace. Either he was trying to frighten her or attempting to polish her off altogether.'

Robert slumped back in his armchair and closed his eyes. 'I probably shouldn't disclose this, Alice, because I made a statement to the police in confidence when they were seeking witnesses. But from my upstairs front window, I saw Andrew approaching her on your tea terrace just after you'd gone up the high street that day. I have no idea what they were saying. I just put it down to Andrew making a move on her. Trying to chat her up, I mean, rather than to assault her. Same as he does to every other unattached woman who passes through Little Pride. He fancies himself as James Bond – irresistible to women. He's even put it about in the village that he's a former spy. He isn't, by the way. He's a retired chartered accountant.'

The memory of how easily I'd got into conversation with Andrew on our first encounter at the bus stop made me nauseous. I grabbed my sherry glass and took another sip to sweeten the acid taste in my mouth.

'I think he must have been trying to silence her about the discovery of the mosaic.'

'But he knew I suspected there was a mosaic there too, and he didn't attempt to shut me up in any way.'

Robert pressed his lips together before speaking. 'Maybe silencing Felicity Stride was a higher priority, because of her position with the council. I'm just glad he must have been interrupted before he could finish poor Felicity off.'

We were both silent as we digested the implications of what Robert had witnessed.

'Now I realise he's the most likely person in the village to have killed Barnaby too,' I said slowly. 'I remember now, I saw Andrew pocketing a few of the tesserae when Barnaby brought them into my shop. I didn't think anything of it at the time, but he must have twigged what they were, and that's what put him onto the existence of the mosaic beneath the paddock, and the possibility that with a little collusion from Magnus, he might be able to steal it. And if they were able to lift and remove a heavy, delicate mosaic without anyone noticing, it would have been the work of moments to whisk poor Barnaby's body away from the building site and bury it in

Maudie's compost heap. So, who do we call first? Felicity Stride or the police?'

Robert considered for a moment. 'If you asked an antiquarian, they might say Felicity. Of course, preserving the mosaic if they haven't already damaged it beyond repair is important, but Andrew's attack on Felicity and the murder of Barnaby surely trump theft of ancient artefacts in terms of criminality. I'll call 999 first, then we'll get on to Felicity, who can fill in the police about the heritage aspect of Robert's offence.'

'Will you call them straight away?' I was desperate for closure.

'Yes, I'll do it right now, before Andrew and Magnus can cover up what they've done. Although there's not much Andrew can do to hide the evidence that won't take hours, even with Magnus doing the heavy lifting. They can hardly return the mosaic to its original site now without it being obvious.'

I grinned. 'My guess is that they're busy with spades and shovels trying to bury it beneath Andrew's lawn. They had the foresight to cut turves from the lawn before digging the trench, but even if they managed to bury it and relay the turves before the police arrive, it will be obvious that the lawn's been disturbed recently.'

'Yes, and it'll take weeks for the ground to settle back to its previous level because digging the soil up will have aerated it. Same principle applies to digging graves. You can't install a headstone for months after a burial, because you have to wait for the ground to settle.'

I gazed into my sherry. Poor Robert, he must have learned that when they buried his late wife.

'But if Andrew was Felicity's attacker,' I queried, 'why was he the one to raise the alarm? Surely he'd have fled the scene to avoid incriminating himself?'

'Perhaps that was exactly what he was thinking. That if he raised the alarm, no one would think for a moment that he could have been her assailant. It would be like an arsonist calling the fire brigade. Sadly, it's not unprecedented for the perpetrator to try to hide their guilt by playing an active part in the investigation of a crime – the murderous husband presenting as the heartbroken widow, and so on. Andrew was probably hoping he'd done enough harm to at least frighten Felicity off. Whatever else he is, he's not stupid. So, speaking of the police, let's get on to them now.'

Everything was falling into place. That was why Andrew had pocketed a few sample tesserae in my shop. He was no casual shoplifter; he wanted to take them away to verify their authenticity before implementing his arrogant plan to steal the mosaic and install it in his own back garden. Andrew would also have benefited from Barnaby's death, because Barnaby was the only other person who seemed to know about the mosaic. With him out of the picture, it would remain a secret. Andrew would also have wanted Felicity off the scene, as she of all people would have instantly recognised the mosaic's significance and value. For the first time, I wondered whether I was next on his hit-list, and the hairs on the back of my neck stood up like an angry porcupine's spines.

As Robert pulled his phone from his pocket, I leaned back against the sofa and closed my eyes, steeling myself to speak to the police. Even though I wanted Andrew and Magnus brought to justice, and the mosaic preserved in its rightful place and the site properly excavated by archaeologists who knew what they were doing, I was not keen to have any more dealings with the police until I knew the fate of my driving licence.

On the other hand, I thought, brightening, *perhaps it'll be a case of third time lucky.*

34

LICENSED TO STAY

It was almost ten o'clock before I returned to my cottage after sharing an impromptu supper at Robert's house. Earlier, Robert and I had returned in his Morgan to lurk just along the high street from the Big House, to watch the police arrive and lead the guilty parties away. If Andrew saw us, he would have recognised Robert's distinctive vehicle, but he stared straight ahead as the police led him in handcuffs to the awaiting panda car. Magnus, following with another officer behind, just looked at the ground, clearly bewildered.

When I called Felicity on her personal mobile, she picked up straight away and was gleeful to hear my account of the evening's proceedings. I omitted Robert's evidence of Andrew as her attacker. I'd leave that for the police to investigate, as we had no proof, but I was confident the police would find Andrew's DNA on her scarf that could not be accounted for in any other way. He must have bought it from Coralie's when she cut his hair. I hoped he hadn't been planning to use it to implicate Coralie in the attack.

Meanwhile, the yellow crime scene tape that now sealed off Andrew's drive, and the police constable posted to guard it while the SOCO team set to work in the back garden, must have set local tongues wagging.

Later, after returning home alone, as I opened my front door, a brown manila envelope lying on the mat made my heart sink. I guessed it was the official letter about the police case against me revealing the results of my blood test at last. What terrible timing!

I closed the front door behind me and leaned against it, trying to build up the courage to open the envelope. I tried to put the matter in perspective. Whatever lay inside could not be a greater threat to my well-being than the one I'd received from Andrew earlier that evening. A driving ban and a fine was nothing compared to Andrew clouting me on the head with his shovel and burying my lifeless body in his back garden.

Taking a deep breath, I ripped the top of the envelope with such force that I tore the letter in half. After reassembling it, I read the few lines of print with trembling hands. This was the gist of the letter:

Dear Miss Carroll,

The recent blood test revealed zero alcohol content, but conclusive evidence of an illegal substance associated with the crime of drink spiking. In consequence, no charge will be made against yourself, but if you have any information regarding anyone who may have been responsible for such an attack and you wish us to take action against them, please contact the number below.

My drink was spiked? I didn't think that sort of thing happened to women of my age, only to younger, more attractive people. I could hardly believe it.

When ABBA burst into song in my jeans pocket, I pulled out my phone and pressed the green button without even looking to see who it was.

'Hi, Alice, it's me, Danny. Good news. Your car's now been fixed, and I picked it up on my way home from work tonight. Martin's offered to follow me out to your house in his car so I can drop it off, and to drive me home again. That'll save you the bother of coming to ours to collect it. Isn't that kind of him?'

Yes, it was uncharacteristically kind of him, when usually it was all he could do to be civil to me.

'Oh yes, thank you, Danny, and thanks to Martin too,' I murmured, distracted by a memory just returning about the post-redundancy drinks. The only person other than Danny to buy me a drink that night was Martin, who bought me not one, but three. I assumed at the time he was just feeling sorry for me.

Martin had always been jealous of my friendship with Danny and was probably glad that I was off the scene at the museum. I suspected he was also insecure in his own relationship with him. Privately, Myrtle and I had agreed Martin was punching above his weight when he started dating Danny.

Now I realised the real reason for Martin's supposed generosity towards me that night.

'By the way, Danny,' I began, choosing my words carefully. 'I've just had a letter from the police saying I wasn't drunk that night but drugged. Someone spiked my drink. That's why I suddenly came over all peculiar on the drive home.'

Danny gasped. 'Well, it wasn't me. You know I'd never do something like that.'

I heard Martin hiss in the background, 'What's up, Danny?'

Danny, in his innocence, said in an aside, 'It's Alice', before returning his attention to me.

'No, I know you wouldn't,' I said quickly. 'Don't worry. But do you know who else was supplying me with drinks that night?'

When I heard a door slam on his end, I realised Martin must have overheard and fled the room in panic.

The line went silent for a moment.

'It was Martin,' I said. 'I think he just couldn't wait to be shot of me. I'm sorry, Danny. I wouldn't be saying this if I wasn't absolutely sure it was true.'

'Why would he do anything to hurt you? And how come he just happened to have a supply of whatever it was he doped you with in his pocket?'

But I could tell by his tone that my accusation rang true. Like me, he was probably wondering whether Martin had ever done anything like this before, and, if not stopped, whether he'd do it again.

'Blimey, no wonder he was angry when I told him I was going to see you home. He must have realised he'd put my life at risk as well as yours, but he was too cowardly to confess.'

I paused. I wasn't done yet, but what I had to say next was going to be even harder.

'The letter from the police says I should tell them if I have any suspects. I'm sorry, Danny, but think I must press charges against Martin.'

I felt wretched for potentially wrecking either their relationship or ours, although it was hardly my fault. In fact, I was probably doing Danny a kindness to alert him to Martin's true nature, and stopping Martin before he could do anything worse.

Danny was way ahead of me. 'And to think I only just moved in with him as well! I can't stay here now. Martin's just gone out – scared of a confrontation with me about this, I guess. As soon as we finish this call, I'm going to grab my things, chuck them in your car and do a runner before he gets back. Most of my stuff is still in boxes at my mum's house, where I was storing everything after moved out of my old flat, so it won't take me long. Anyway, I can spend another night with a man who would do that to you. Quite apart from the risk to myself. Who's to say he hasn't got some more of that stuff stashed away somewhere?'

'Where will you go? To your mum's?'

'I suppose so, although only as a temporary respite. She's long since turned my old bedroom into a study for her academic work. I'll have to sleep on her sofa.'

His voice contorted with misery, and my heart went out to him.

'I've got a spare bedroom, Danny,' I blurted, without thinking it through. 'You're welcome to stay with me until you find your own place again, if you don't mind sharing it with some of Nell Little's clutter.'

'That would be wonderful, Alice, thank you. I'll start looking for a place of my own straight away, I promise. I won't cramp your newly single style. It's going to be really awkward at work, though, what with Martin being ever-present and higher grade than me. Maybe I'll have to resign.'

'No, you mustn't. When I press charges, they won't be able to keep him on at the museum in a public-facing job. If he doesn't quit of his own volition, he'll be forced out soon enough.'

Danny gave a huge sigh. Poor Danny, it was a lot to process. All he'd expected from this phone call was the pleasure of telling me my car was fixed.

'I'll pay you rent, of course,' he added.

Hurrah, another source of income, I thought, before scolding myself for being mercenary.

'It's the least I can do, Danny. After all, you probably saved my life when you offered to see me home that night.'

Danny wouldn't let that go. 'Actually, you have the police to thank for that, for pulling you over when you were driving errati-cally. But at least you can sleep easy now knowing you did nothing wrong, and you can still drive. And now you know you're not to blame for not being able to remember much the next morning either. The doping explains it all.'

That was a comforting thought.

'It's odd, though, a few little snippets have been filtering back into my head since then. Just now, I had a sudden memory of doing karaoke to an ABBA song in the pub that night. Did I really do that? You know my voice isn't up to much. I even used to mouth the words when we were singing "Happy Birthday" to people in the office.'

The warmth in Danny's voice told me he was grinning. I was glad to have cheered him up. 'I'm afraid you did, Alice. Now that really was criminal.'

ACKNOWLEDGEMENTS

I've very much enjoyed researching and writing this story, the first in a new series of cozy mystery novels. I am grateful to Alison Morton, author of the *Roma Nova* alternative history novels for her infectious enthusiasm and detailed knowledge about the Ancient Romans; to the Corinium Museum in Cirencester for its wonderful display of Roman mosaics and its helpful staff; and to Dr Angela Buckley, crime historian and author, for her knowledge of Victorian medicine bottles, many of which I've dug up in my own Cotswold garden over the years.

As ever, huge thanks to the brilliant team at Boldwood Books for polishing my manuscript as thoroughly as Alice spring-cleaned her Cotswold Curiosity Shop and for sending it out into the world so beautifully packaged. I can't wait to share more of Alice's adventures.

ABOUT THE AUTHOR

Debbie Young is the much-loved author of the Sophie Sayers and St Brides cosy crime mysteries. She lives in a Cotswold village, where she runs the local literary festival, and has worked at Westonbirt School, both of which provide inspiration for her writing.

Sign up to Debbie Young's mailing list for news, competitions and updates on future books.

Visit Debbie's Website: www.authordebbieyoung.com

Follow Debbie on social media:

 x.com/DebbieYoungBN

facebook.com/AuthorDebbieYoung

bookbub.com/authors/debbie-young

instagram.com/debbieyoungauthor

ALSO BY DEBBIE YOUNG

A Gemma Lamb Cozy Mystery

Dastardly Deeds at St Bride's

Sinister Stranger at St Bride's

Wicked Whispers at St Bride's

Artful Antics at St Bride's

A Sophie Sayers Cozy Mystery

Murder at the Vicarage

Best Murder in Show

Murder in the Manger

Murder at the Well

Springtime for Murder

Murder at the Mill

Murder Lost and Found

Murder in the Highlands

Driven to Murder

The Cotswold Curiosity Shop Mysteries

Death at the Old Curiosity Shop

Poison
& Pens

POISON & PENS IS THE HOME OF
COZY MYSTERIES SO POUR YOURSELF
A CUP OF TEA & GET SLEUTHING!

DISCOVER PAGE-TURNING NOVELS FROM
YOUR FAVOURITE AUTHORS &
MEET NEW FRIENDS

JOIN OUR
FACEBOOK GROUP

BIT.LYPOISONANDPENSFB

SIGN UP TO OUR
NEWSLETTER

BIT.LY/POISONANDPENSNEWS

Boldwood

Milton Keynes UK
Ingram Content Group UK Ltd.
UKHW040635241024
2353UKWH00044B/377